KNOCK OFF THE HAT
A CLIFFORD WATERMAN GAY PHILLY MYSTERY

RICHARD STEVENSON

AMBLE
PRESS
ANN ARBOR

2022

Amble Press

Print ISBN: 978-1-61294-231-5

Bywater Books First Edition: April 2022

Printed in the United States of America on acid-free paper.

Cover design by TreeHouse Studio

Amble Press
PO Box 3671
Ann Arbor MI 48106-3671

www.amblepressbooks.com

KNOCK OFF THE HAT

A CLIFFORD WATERMAN GAY PHILLY MYSTERY

CHAPTER 1

"It smells like something died in here," Byron Summerson sniffed, getting things between us off to a not-great start.

"That's just my lunch."

"I had thought if I successfully navigated the Twentieth Street tunnel without tossing my cookies I'd be home free in the olfactory sense. But such, it seems, is not to be. I was told that you are effective in your investigative work, Mr. Waterman, but I have to say I am quite astonished that you require a prospective client to traverse Satan's maw itself in order to arrive at your headquarters. And then when that possible paying customer has actually managed to set foot inside the premises, he is all but overcome by the stench of I can't imagine what."

I guessed he was around my age, forty-three. He'd dressed suitably for the heat of Philadelphia in August in lightweight nicely pressed slacks and a baby blue cotton sports shirt that matched the color of his watery eyes. He had a Sears catalog underwear model's pleasantly bland face, and a build that was, like mine, just starting to thicken.

"My apologies, Mr. Summerson, but my fan croaked yesterday. Not that the thing clears the air in here all that much even when it's running."

I forced a grin but he didn't force one back. We both

noted the inert machine on top of my file cabinet. Its blades were shiny with what was probably some kind of oil, though more likely cooking than machine. The exhaust fan from Ted's Luncheonette was three floors below my window, a hazard this time of year that I was used to. But rising fryolator haze was something Byron Summerson was unlikely to have had to adapt to out in Spic and Span Chestnut Hill.

"We can all be grateful," Summerson went on, "that the railroad is going to take down that dreadful Chinese wall. A person is lucky to make his way underneath it without being murdered or simply slipping and falling in a pool of urine or worse. And then on top of all that—oh my, the soot!"

He indicated the open window with the adjustable screen I had jammed into the aperture. The thing was black with residue from the Pennsylvania Railroad steam locomotives that chugged by my building on the way to or from Broad Street Station every couple of minutes. Sometimes new clients mistook my unshaven look for soot from the engines, but the black stubble on my face was just something hereditary, I occasionally had to explain.

"I know it's hot in here," I said. "May I order up a cold 7Up or something?"

"I think a Coke if you please."

He looked perplexed when I reached for the phone and dialed Ted's. "This won't take but a minute. They're not that busy midafternoon."

I wrenched the screen out of the window and lowered the plywood box and length of clothesline that the office's previous tenant—an oilcloth sales agent who never made it back from the Solomon Islands—had rigged up in order to retrieve drinks and meals from Ted's back door.

"I hauled up a couple of growlers for lunch," I said. "They didn't smell all that bad at the time."

Now Summerson looked as if he might bolt any second, a development to be averted, if possible, inasmuch as my light bill was already two weeks overdue and the phone company was likewise in a pre-pounce crouch. I leaned back in my swivel chair—it squeaked twice, groaned once—and said, "You told me on the phone you wanted to inquire about my handling a situation on behalf of a friend. Who's the friend, and what's the situation?"

He was still looking queasy. "What in heaven's name is a growler?"

"It's a dog from Ted's with his famous Texas chili sauce."

"Famous? Given the odor it leaves, may I suggest *infamous* would be the more appropriate word for it?"

The guy was getting on my nerves. I flipped a Lucky out of the pack in my shirt pocket and fired it up.

"That's actually quite an attractive ashtray," Summerson said, indicating the object I dropped the match into. "Or would be attractive if its rim wasn't thick with oozing toxic substances. Is it Indian brass?"

"It's Egyptian. Anyway, that's where I bought it, in a souk. It's a souvenir of my tenure as a United States Army MP in Cairo."

Now he examined me almost approvingly. "So, you worked with British intelligence? That must have been fascinating—and, I should think, quite important to the war effort."

"Actually, I was working with US Army *un*intelligence. There was a whole lot of that going on, in case you haven't heard. It's lucky the Japs and the Nazis were even dumber."

"I have indeed heard from many that that was the case."

"My job," I went on, "was keeping the few American GIs who hadn't shipped across the Mediterranean to join the fight from having too nice a time while their buddies were getting shot at up in Europe. Like busting soldiers for smoking hashish out of a glass coffeepot, or grabbing belly dancers' veils, or what have you. When I enlisted, it's what the army in its lack of wisdom decided I'd be good at."

3

The 3:12 from Harrisburg chuff-chuffed by, its engine's sulfurous fumes wafting through the window like a breeze from Lucifer.

"But, Mr. Waterman, I was told you had been a police officer prior to your military service. So wasn't an MP designation altogether suitable?"

"I had just made detective here in Philly before I went in, but I wasn't investigating crimes in Egypt. I was rounding up drunks and dope fiends. And quite a few perverts too, of course, so they could be properly cashiered and told to scram on back to East Jesus."

Summerson frowned at either the fact or the language. "I should think that must have been hard for you—what with your being that way yourself."

The clothesline wobbled. I leaned over and tugged up the box with the two bottles of pop, my 7Up, and Summerson's Coke. I had put a quarter in the box, and I snatched up my fifteen cents change. If somehow Summerson wasn't going to work out as a client, I'd need the extra cash.

I said, "See that?"

I directed Summerson's attention to a framed certificate I'd hung on the wall in a dim corner of the office.

He squinted and said, "I can't read it from here. What is it?"

"It's my discharge from the Armed Forces of the United States of America under other than honorable conditions."

"Oh, my word."

"Nobody mentioned this to you, Byron? It's known around town. It's the reason I didn't go back to the cops after the war."

I handed him his Coke. He took it but didn't drink. "No, I wasn't told."

"I'm relieved my name comes up for anything else." I sucked in some more scratchy reassurance from my smoldering Lucky.

"So you were—what? Arrested for one of the offenses you yourself were arresting others for? How perfectly dreadful!"

I thought about adding a little Kickapoo flavoring to my 7Up from the bottle in my desk drawer but had the sense to wait until Summerson left a cash deposit.

"You'd never know it from the recruiting posters," I told him, "but the army does have a flair for irony. I was turned in by a fellow investigative officer who came back to our room one night while I was enjoying the company of a nice man named Idriss, who normally cleaned the latrines. On this particular occasion, this pleasant chappie was cleaning *my* latrine, and that didn't go over well with my commanding officer when he heard about it."

Summerson clung to the Coke bottle he was holding and was looking a bit green around the gills again. "My, my. You seem to have a taste for the exotic, Mr. Waterman. An Arab, for goodness' sake. Like T.E. Lawrence."

"The report said something to the effect of, 'Sergeant Waterman was discovered in the act of being buggered by a wog.' A week later I was on a ship home."

Summerson seemed to ruminate over this for a moment, took a delicate swig of his Coke and came to a conclusion. "In that case, I think you are just the man to take on a situation involving a similar injustice. You were obviously helpless in the face of the army's cruelty and stupidity, but perhaps you can find a way to deal successfully with a lesser institution. Are you familiar with a Philadelphia magistrate who is generally referred to by the sobriquet 'The Hat'?"

I thought, *oh hell.*

CHAPTER 2

Judge Harold Stetson was the one magistrate you really did not want to appear before if you had been picked up in a bar raid or a Rittenhouse Square roundup for "disorderly conduct"—that is, being a homosexual. It was pay-to-play in his courtroom. You either paid up or got the max, which included public humiliation along with a hefty fine or even jail time. Nicknamed for the headgear he wore on the street and which coincidentally bore his family name, the judge had arranged for most of the court system's "homo" cases to be sent his way. Nobody knew which thrilled him more, the suffering he inflicted on Philadelphia's "inverts" or the cash flow from the extortion racket he ran.

I said, "Don't tell me you're being dragged into Stetson's courtroom. My deepest sympathy, if that's the case."

Summerson gulped his Coke. A Sudan-shaped sweat stain had appeared in the right underarm of what, when he had first entered the office, had looked like a freshly laundered shirt. I had changed shirts just after noon, but the temperature in the room must have been over ninety. The Schuylkill River, a couple of blocks away, might as well have been the Nile.

"It is not I who must face The Hat," Summerson said, "but my friend Leslie Croyer. Leslie was one of the unfortunates arrested Monday night during the police raid at Stem t' Stern.

I'm guessing you've heard about that perfectly absurd attack. Perhaps you were in attendance yourself and escaped out the back door, as a few entirely innocent imbibers managed to do."

Not far from my office, Stem t' Stern, usually just called "Stem," was a gay bar on Cuthbert Street with a vaguely nautical motif, though the *double entendre* of the moniker was as well understood by the hostile authorities as it was by the tavern's regular customers.

"I wasn't there. I mainly hang out over at Sal's. But I read the story in the *Inquirer* this morning."

"Ah, yes. 'Police Nab Fourteen Degenerates in Raid on Club.' At least no names were listed in the paper. At least not yet."

"No, the newsies are probably waiting for a conviction or guilty pleas before they plaster the unlucky perps' names all over town. The Hat will see to that."

"The thing of it is," Summerson said, reddening a bit and pale eyes shining, "Leslie simply cannot afford to have this preposterous matter go forward. No conviction, no name in the paper. No record whatsoever. Leslie believes his life would be destroyed, and I believe he is absolutely right about that. The whole thing is just so—*so ridiculously unfair.*"

"I know."

"He'd lose his job at MacPherson Insurance. It happened to an acquaintance of ours, Todd Ferguson. The day after he was arrested, his supervisor learned what had taken place from an attorney friend and Todd was just *out*. He's working at a gas station now in Reading, I'm told, and barely subsisting."

"It stinks."

"The thing about Leslie is . . ." Summerson's voice broke. I waited while he collected himself. I tried to shoot my cigarette smoke off to the side, but with the fan sitting uselessly on its perch, the smoke just hung in the air between us. Another train crept by seventy-five feet away spewing hot gasses. The Pennsy was only just beginning to transition from steam to diesel locomotives, and for now the year might as well have been 1917 instead of 1947 on the Chinese wall, the line's old granite viaduct carrying passenger traffic into Center City and all but splitting the city in half.

"I'm afraid," Summerson went on, "that if Leslie were to have his name listed in the newspaper as an arrestee in a gay raid, he might do something—well, something . . . something desperate."

"You mean kill himself? It won't help to not say it."

"He is emotionally quite fragile. The probable job loss would be plenty bad enough. But on top of that, even worse, there's his family. They don't know about Leslie, and up in Lock Haven, where he's from, people read the *Inquirer*. He says his parents would be devastated if it came out that he was gay, and the entire Croyer family would be incredibly embarrassed."

"Embarrassed? That's the word you use if you have toilet paper stuck to your shoe."

He looked at me imploringly. "I'm sure you know what I mean."

"I guess I do."

"So the thing of it is, we are prepared to do what needs to be done to—as Judge Stetson's court clerk phrased it—make this thing simply go away."

"Uh huh."

"He talked to me the way gangsters talk in the movies."

"Fairly often in real life too, you seem shocked to discover."

"Not shocked, really. Every gay man in Philadelphia knows how the entirely corrupt system works for gay people. But, you see, here's the thing . . ."

He blushed again, the sweat on his brow gleaming even under the sixty watts' worth of amber light that made everybody who came in and sat down wonder if they shouldn't be checked out for malaria.

"The thing is, it's the current economics of it," Summerson

said. "Leslie hasn't a lot of money. I mean, essentially none whatsoever beyond his weekly paycheck."

"No contingency funds. I get that."

"And neither, I am sorry to say, am I awash in a reserve of funds. I am bordering on penniless, to get right to the crux of it."

"Is Croyer your boyfriend?" I asked.

He slumped a bit, and his face suddenly looked a few years older than when he came in. "No, Leslie is not my lover. I admit to you, Mr. Waterman, that I wish he were. We had one quasi-erotic interlude after we chatted in Rittenhouse Square on May 7. But Leslie is twenty years younger than I am, and he sees me as more of an avuncular figure. I've had to accept the fact that he considers me a bit over the hill for love."

I was trying to imagine what a "quasi-erotic interlude" looked like, but without much luck.

"So you two don't live together?"

"I reside in the guest cottage of what at one time was my family's Chestnut Hill estate, and since early July Leslie has resided in the chauffeur's apartment over the garage. I rent the main house to the principal owner of Supreme Markets and his family, and the income from the rental allows me to cover the estate's taxes and upkeep. My parents and grandparents lived in the house previously until the prewar economy led to a reversal of fortune. It's a sad story you have no doubt heard before."

I said I had.

"Mummy and Daddy currently make their home near my sister Lorna and her husband in Mechanicsburg. Daddy was a vice president for the railroad and retired with a great deal of depressed stock but not a sizable pension, so his cash reserves are also limited. Not that, in any event, he would ever consider rendering financial assistance to a lad with whom his son yearns to share illicit physical intimacy."

I was still working on "quasi-erotic."

I said, "So where might I come in, Mr. Summerson? And

9

can you afford me? I charge forty-five dollars a day and expenses. I try to keep the expenses down, but if you want a good result, you never know."

He nodded. "I was told of your entirely reasonable fee schedule. I can afford that for at least a short time. I do enjoy a modest income from my small business of buying and selling antique reticules."

What were those? Something for trimming your fingernails? I said, "Okay, good."

"So, do you think you can do it?"

"Do what? Help me out. I can't read your mind."

"Why, negotiate a lower payoff."

"To The Hat?"

"And his clerk. I was told by acquaintances that the normal charge for expunging the records in a case of Leslie's type would be fifty dollars. But when I met the clerk, Ray Phipps, on the steps of the courthouse yesterday morning, he told me the price had gone up. It's now five hundred dollars. I told him that was preposterous and Leslie could in no way afford to lay out such a huge amount. Do you know what he replied?"

"What?"

"He told me I should complain to the Better Business Bureau."

Something was screwy here. The fifty figure sounded right. Five hundred sounded wrong. *Preposterous* was exactly the word for it.

"I can check it out," I said, and a glimmer of something less tropical-disease-like passed over Summerson's face.

"But," I said, "it's pretty certain your friend is going to have to pay something. Justice for gay people in Philadelphia isn't going to come cheap for the foreseeable future, if ever. Has Leslie hired a lawyer?"

"Gary Trask. It was he who suggested I solicit your help. It was Mr. Trask's belief that someone of your experience and connections was what was needed under this peculiar set of circumstances. He assured me that you are a man who knows people."

"Knows people is good; is known *by* people is less good. But in a thing like this, there are limits."

"Well, just do what you can."

"Is it possible you misunderstood Phipps, and the figure he actually quoted you was fifty dollars?"

"No, he was entirely clear in his quotation. He asked me to stick my arm out. Then he raised my sleeve, and he wrote on my arm with some kind of black grease pencil the figure 500. I had a devil of a time trying to wash it off, in fact."

Summerson rolled up his right sleeve and displayed for me the still visible figure in two-inch-high numbering beginning with a dollar sign.

The 3:50 to Pittsburgh rumbled by, and again I thought, *What the hell is going on here?*

CHAPTER 3

Over on Spruce Street was a seedy rooming house where a group of us kept a hideaway for "quasi-erotic" and various other purposes. What you did was, you called up the owner of the building, a sometime drag queen who went by Florence Anderson when she wasn't being Forrest Anderson, and asked if the room was available for an hour. If it was, you'd go in the main entrance and whoever you were meeting generally came in the back from an alley.

That afternoon, when I'd finished my business with Summerson, I called Anderson, got the all clear and went in through the front door. Bobby Carletti had entered from the rear. I met him on the second-floor landing, both of us jangling keys to room seven. I opened it with mine.

Room seven had a double bed with noisy springs and what felt like a big sack of hot mashed potatoes for a mattress. There was a couch and a kitchen table, but no kitchen, just a hot plate with a frayed cord one of the regulars had wrapped electrical tape around. On an end table sat a white Bakelite radio normally tuned to the station that carried the Phillies games.

Bobby was out of his Philadelphia Police Department uniform and dressed for the heat in lightweight slacks and a navy blue T. A little older than I was, the cop was in better shape.

12

He'd wrestled at Morristown High and tried to stay trim. There were no growlers on Bobby's breath when I kissed him, just the pleasantly acrid howdy-do of his two-pack-a-day Old Golds habit. He sometimes joked about being hooked on "coffin nails," and I had to agree that at least what my dad told me when I started smoking at age eleven was true, that cigarettes could stunt your growth.

"Were you able to get the list?" I asked him.

"Piece of cake."

I poured a Jim Beam from the stash I keep in a cabinet and Bobby got himself a Carling's from the six-pack he kept in the ancient canister-topped fridge we'd found in the cellar and dragged up the stairs. The window overlooking Spruce was open, but there was no cross-ventilation. The oscillating fan on top of the cabinet was functioning, though, and Bobby switched on its back-and-forth deranged routine of turning this way and that way.

I took a seat at the table and looked over the list of everybody who had been arrested at Stem t' Stern on Monday night. Bobby sat across from me, relaxing with an Old Gold and enjoying his brew.

"How come they hit the place on a Monday?" I wondered. "Eighteen guys is hardly worth the bother once the proceeds are divided up among the judge, the courtroom staff, the bail bondsmen, and the precinct captain."

"I wouldn't know. Those decisions are made outside of my earshot."

"Why not on the weekend? How many people are in there on a Friday or Saturday night? Fifty? Seventy-five? A hundred?"

Carletti had black eyelashes that curved out and up about a foot, and they fluttered in a way that always stimulated my attention.

"Who knows? I mean, why not during the week? Maybe it's not for filthy lucre this time but just for fun. Scare a bar full of fairies and make 'em run around and squeak."

I thought I recognized a few names on the list in addition to Leslie Croyer.

"Terry Jennings. Doesn't he work for the archdiocese? If they hear tell, his employers are going to be awfully disappointed."

"His employers and his confessor. The guy'll be counting Hail Marys till the Phils win the pennant."

"And Tom Heimer. I know the name from somewhere. Didn't he have a big crush on Monnie Hinkle, and Monnie practically had to go into hiding to get rid of the bozo?"

"Tom's a dinge queen, so, yeah, could be."

Not being prejudiced, I didn't like that term, but I wasn't about to get into it with Bobby.

"Amos Leary I've met, a nice guy. What rotten luck he got caught in the anti-pansy dragnet. These other people I don't know. Do you?"

"No, but I don't get around town the way you do, Clifford, not to the bar scene anyway. I'm ID'd in a fag bar and I'm fucked nine ways to Sunday. Unless I'm the arrester instead of the arrestee, of course. But I try to stay away from those assignments."

I had sometimes wondered about this. "Have you ever taken part in a raid? Actually had to nab guys you maybe knew? Or even fucked? Jesus."

He fingered his bottle of Carling's and shrugged. "Never a bar, nah, but a couple of times in Rittenhouse Square. It was around election time and word was we had to clean the place up, make the degenerates hide out in New Hope till after the mayor got back in. This one time I thought a guy recognized me, but I gave him the stink eye and convinced him he was seeing things. But, hey, I really don't approve of that crap, and I stay as far away from it as I can."

The list of arrestees in front of me had home addresses, work addresses, and phone numbers. Most of them lived in Center City, but a few were in West Philly, one was from Haverford,

14

and one from Cherry Hill, over in Jersey.

"If you can," I told Bobby, "ask around and get the skinny on the price of gay get-out-of-jail payoffs inflating ten times over."

"Phipps really told your client he'd have to cough up five hundred bucks?"

"I saw it in writing, and it stinks. Can you find out if this is a one-off, or what? It has to be. It can't be sustained. There aren't enough gay millionaires in Philadelphia to keep it going. Maybe in New York, but not here in our sleepy little metropolis-in-size-only hick burg."

"What can you do for this guy anyway?" Bobby asked. "He's screwed, and that's that. He forks over the big ones, or he pays the smaller fine and gets his name in the *Inquirer* pervy-bar debutante announcements. Why're you taking on a loser of a case like that?"

"I need the forty-five a day, for one. Anyway, I'm curious about what the hell this is all about. It's cockamamie."

"You hurting for business? How come? Is it seasonal or what?"

"I had a couple of ugly divorce gigs last month that paid the bills. Plus a junior high thing in Hatboro where the cafeteria manager had her hand in the till so she could shower her eighth-grade boyfriend with sports memorabilia and alcoholic beverages. There was a missing granddad situation last week in Germantown. But the old guy had just hitched a ride down to Atlantic City to see if there was still a horse that dives off a tower into a tub of water. He'd told a pal down at the Odd Fellows where he was going, so I had him back to his pissed-off daughter in under twenty-four hours."

Bobby chuckled. "Of course there's still a diving horse on Steel Pier. Did Gramps get to watch it? My kids couldn't believe it when we went last year."

"We both enjoyed the spectacle, and then I drove him back home."

15

"That car of yours made it all the way to the shore and back? Cripes, that's hard to believe."

My faded pea-green prewar Plymouth coupe had nearly 86,000 miles on it. I rarely drove the aged tin can very far outside Philly.

I said, "My new client's friend, a down-at-the-heels former aristocrat from Chestnut Hill—he sells vestibules or something—advanced me two days' fees, so I'm going to do whatever I can. Thanks for getting me going."

"You know I'm always happy to get you going, Clifford," Bobby said, and reached across the table, grabbing me by the hair. His pitch-black hair was as curly as mine was straight and harder to get hold of, but I could get him by the ears, and did. Bobby was into fresh sweat—something to do with his high school wrestling days in Morristown—so for the next half hour or so he was in for a real feast.

CHAPTER 4

Even before I met Amos Leary at seven in Horn & Hardart's for dinner, I learned of some very strange goings-on. Making a few calls, I found out that somebody in the cops had tipped off the owner of Polly-Wolly's, a gay bar just up the street from Stem, that another raid was in the works and to beware.

I asked the tavern's owner, Nelson Miller, what "beware" was supposed to mean, and what was he meant to do? He said he had no idea, and anyway he was skeptical of the report. He told me he didn't think another bar would be hit so soon. He thought the police would likely wait until the saloon-going regulars had let down their guard and the potential roundup numbers were monetarily worthwhile again. I asked him who his police informant was, but he wouldn't say. It wouldn't have been Bobby, who was too low ranking to be in on plans of that type—or so Bobby always claimed.

In my head I sometimes questioned Bobby's credibility. In addition to his sometime sweaty-sex-with-guys habit, he had a wife and four boys in the row house where he lived up near Shibe Park. Two of his boys were in a new thing called Little League, where the kids stayed on a team, wore uniforms, and the parents were involved—all of which sounded like asking for trouble, though Bobby said the kids seemed to like it. Guys who lived lives this complicated were generally not to be trusted, and with Bobby I was never sure.

I talked to a couple of other bar managers, and they were even less forthcoming. Their establishments were mob-owned, I knew, and that afforded them some protection. But it wasn't unknown for certain hoodlums in the City of Brotherly Love to extort large cash sums from their own customers, and this was on top of them watering every drink they served.

I'd met Amos Leary a few times at parties and had been sorry to find him on the list of Stem-raid victims. A cheerful, rotund fellow of fifty or so, he sold shoes at Wanamaker's. He'd had a longtime boyfriend in the Merchant Marine who was on a vessel sunk by a U-boat off Hollywood Beach, Florida, in 1943. His pal hadn't been one of the lucky thirteen survivors. The incident had never made the papers, bad for morale.

Horn and Hardart's automat was pretty crowded for seven o'clock—most Philadelphians were sensible people who liked their supper around six. A steady line moved their cafeteria trays along the meat and potato offerings, and others were dropping coins in the slots and opening the little windows for a ham sandwich or a piece of pie.

When he came through the door, Amos spotted me and tried to smile, that being his nature. I'd left my jacket and tie at the office, Horn & Hardart's supposedly being air-conditioned, but Amos still had his work duds on and wore black loafers that gleamed like the freshly mined anthracite that was carted out of mountains up near Amos's hometown of Mauch Chunk.

I offered Amos a Lucky when he sat down across from me, and he took it.

"How goes it, Clifford? I haven't seen you since that party at Marsha Malinowski's where she told everybody Lauren Bacall was going to drop in and people didn't believe it, and then around midnight Lauren Bacall actually *did* walk in the door—except after she'd had a couple of Manhattans and started flashing people out in the kitchen this Lauren Bacall had a dick as big as Bogie's!"

I hadn't heard that about Bogie—just Roddy McDowell—but I figured Amos probably picked up a lot of reliable information in the shoe department.

I said I remembered that party fondly, if hazily, having passed out on a glider on the hostess's front porch only to awaken on Sunday morning to see families in their spiffiest outfits climbing the front steps of the Presbyterian church across the street.

"Yeah, you were drinking because you were sad," Amos recalled. "I remember we talked that night. I had suffered a loss at the hands of the arch-fiend Adolf Hitler, and so had you."

I had no memory of this. "I'm not sure who you mean. In my case, I mean."

He dragged contentedly on his Lucky despite a distant rattling sound at the back of his throat whenever he exhaled. "You said his name was Duane. I remember that because I have a second cousin Duane and it's kind of an unusual name. You said he was killed in the Pacific and he was your—I remember distinctly you using the words *first love*."

"I'm not sure I didn't give you a wrong impression, Amos. Duane Peavey wasn't ever a lover of mine. He was a kid in eleventh grade who fell asleep against me on the bus coming back from a football game against Bethlehem. He was breathing on my neck and I got a raging bone on. I consider this my first sexual experience with a male, but maybe *first love* is not quite the right term."

He chuckled. "That's what you called him at Marsha's party, but you weren't as sober as you are now. So that must explain it."

Memories suddenly flooded back to my actual first love—a gratifying interlude and then a fiasco—but that was nothing to either be flippant about or hash over at Horn & Hardart's on a hot summer night with more pressing matters at hand.

"Speaking of raising a glass or four," I said, "it's really rotten that you all got busted at Stem on Monday. Was it your first time?"

He struggled to maintain his cheery outlook but couldn't.

"Oh, I've had a number of run-ins with Alice Blue. Once in Fairmount Park, another time in a tearoom on the Broad Street line. But it was the first time I was actually arrested and not just shooed away. A couple of guys got out the back door in time, but I don't move that fast and an athletic young patrolman I'd have loved to take home cuffed me and shoved me in the wagon before I had a chance to convince the lad he was going to miss out on a real treat."

"He'll never know."

"The first thing I thought was, uh oh, my boss at the store. I mean, yeah, he has to know I'm gay. But a hint of mint is one thing and my name in the *Inquirer* in the disgusting degenerates column is something else. And I love working at Wanamaker's. I'm proud to be part of a famous store with such a stellar reputation, and I really just *adore* all the girls I work with."

"Have you told your boss what happened?"

A vigorous shake of the head. "Not a good idea, I found out. I asked Louise in gift wrap what she thought—she worked in shoes till last year. She said Arthur, my supervisor, would probably not put up with me getting my name in the paper as a notorious queer."

"Hell."

"I do *not* want to lose my job, so I did the only thing I *could* do. I think you know what that is."

"Oh no."

"My court date would have been next Tuesday."

"Would have been?"

"On my lunch hour today I walked over to the courthouse and I handed Ray Phipps, The Hat's court clerk, five hundred dollars."

"Jesus. So it's true the payoff rate has gone up."

"I didn't know it had ever been less than five hundred till one of the girls at work told me. It was just . . . unbelievable. But I live in Philly. I have no choice, do I?"

"So, Amos. Has this—what? Wiped out your savings? Or did you have a nest egg put away for a rainy day?"

His gray eyes hardened. "Do you know what I had in my savings account until eleven o'clock this morning? A hundred and eighty dollars."

"So how did you come up with the five hundred? Rob a bank?"

His gaze sank down to the table, and then his hands came up to cover his round face. I heard him say in a muffled voice, "I sold my car."

CHAPTER 5

We both had meat loaf, potatoes, string beans, and a piece of pie. Amos had coconut cream pie and I had lemon meringue. Flush with my retainer from Byron Summerson, I sprang for the eats and Amos said he appreciated the gesture. We didn't live far from each other on Locust, and we walked back over there together on the sizzling streets. I'd recently seen a movie short where Asians walked barefoot on hot coals, but they would have balked at doing the same thing on the pavement around Rittenhouse Square. It was the kind of summer weather where in the city's days of yore yellow fever festered. During the revolution, George Washington slept up in the hills away from the swampy plain and probably sent a slave down to pick up takeout fish muddle and trifle for dessert.

I asked Amos if he would be going back to Stem t' Stern after a cooling off period, but he said not a chance. He planned to stick to private parties for socializing for the foreseeable future. I reminded him that sometimes they got raided, too, if the shrieking level reached a certain pitch and the neighbors complained.

"Cliff," Amos explained, "I am a social animal. I like other people and I need other people. So I'll keep on going out. They forgot to put it in the Constitution, but even as a pathetic queer,

I have the right to do so."

"What rights are you referring to?"

We had stopped in front of his building and he spoke to me in a conversational tone even though passers-by might have taken note of his words. Somebody had a radio on in his building with the window open and I could make out The Harmonicats strolling sweetly through "Peg o' My Heart."

"Ever heard of Karl Heinrich Ulrichs?" Amos asked me.

"The name doesn't ring a bell."

"He was a nineteenth-century German who tried to get the anti-homosexual laws repealed over there. It was a kind of crusade he really devoted his adult life to."

"The guy had balls."

"He called people like us Uranians, a word he made up. He believed our sexual orientation was established by nature, and he said lawmakers had no right to veto nature."

Amos was being so sincere that I didn't make a crack about "your anus."

I said, "I'll bet he didn't make a lot of headway with that particular argument, did he?"

A man who spent his days dealing with people's feet, Amos was patient. "Ulrichs never got the laws changed, but he changed some minds. The logic of what he was saying got through to a number of intelligent people. Unfortunately, what little progress he made was blotted out by the Nazis. They burned his books."

"If it hadn't been Hitler," I said, "it might have been the Philadelphia City Council in an election year."

Amos chuckled, but even in the glow of a single streetlight I could see in his eyes he didn't find what I said even a little bit funny. I wondered if he'd invite me in for a nightcap—needing to make some phone calls and in need of a cold shower, I'd have said no thanks—but Amos simply thanked me for the meat loaf and pie, turned, and walked, I thought, a bit disconsolately into his building.

Five minutes later, up in my apartment with two fans churning, I got out of all my sodden garments, and stood in the tepid flow of the shower until nicotine withdrawal started to gnaw. I dried off, went in the living room, poured some Jim Beam into a Kraft sandwich-spread glass, and placed a stack of Coleman Hawkins records on the changer. "Body and Soul" was always first, and sometimes I'd retrieve it from the pile and play it over again.

In Cairo I'd sometimes paid a boy to wave a palm frond over me while I fell asleep, but here I sat by the window with the two fans substituting for tropical cooling-down practices and sprawled nude on the davenport. I enjoyed my drink and smoked a cigarette. The Hawkins was just the ticket for a sultry night like this in a sultry place like this—or for any other night or place—until the phone rang.

It was Byron Summerson. He said he thought I would want to know that another gay bar had been hit, Polly-Wolly's.

CHAPTER 6

I got dressed and walked over toward the scene of the raid. Passing through Rittenhouse Square, I ran into a couple I knew, Dan Klemenski and Ronald Fine, who said they'd heard about the incident and had a friend who had been arrested. The guy was still at the precinct house at Eleventh and Winter. His boyfriend had gone over to try to bail him out.

"The cops have gone nuts," Fine said, sounding exasperated. "The cops and The Hat. They're charging people five thousand dollars to get the charges dropped, and some people are just going ahead and paying it. I mean, God, it's like some kind of homo genocide or something."

"It won't work," Klemenski insisted. "People will just stay home and the bars will go bankrupt. Then what will those hypocritical courthouse reprobates do? Charging that much, they're killing the goose that lays the golden eggs. Are they really that stupid?"

"I heard it was five hundred, not five thousand," I said. "Not that it makes all that much difference for a lot of people."

"There's definitely something new going on," Klemenski said. "A month ago a couple of the girls got caught in Fairmount Park at two in the morning. They were on a picnic table with one of them heels to Jesus when a vice squad queen with searchlights and a bullhorn snuck up, and the two unfortunates got carted off to the hoosegow. But they were on their way home three hours later, and it only cost them twenty-five each."

"So what is it," Fine wondered, "that all of a sudden it's costing hundreds of dollars to suck dick in Philadelphia?"

It was the question of the week, and I was being paid a reasonable sum to find out the answer.

At Polly-Wolly's, the lights were on inside but there was no other sign of life. An empty squad car was parked in front, engine idling with its red roof-light churning. For a minute, I wondered: what if I just got in and drove the vehicle down Arch Street to the closest pier on the Delaware and gave it a shove?

A small crowd was still gathered, having a look, but they were keeping a safe distance. I kept an eye out for anybody I knew and soon spotted Mary Ann Tate, a dyke who almost got booted out of the armed forces like me. But she had the goods on so many officers they let her stay and then gave her not only an honorable discharge but four or five commendations. She was a slender woman with watchful green eyes and a swirl of straw-colored hair. She had been crowned the Flaming Foliage Queen at her upstate hometown high school when she was seventeen. Now, postwar, she worked for an auto parts wholesaler and lived nearby with her girlfriend, Noreen.

"Hey, Cliff," she said, smiling, "if you came over here to get arrested for sodomitical practices, you're too late. The paddy wagon pulled out forty-five minutes ago."

"I heard."

"They got Stem on Monday. What is it with this particular street that all of a sudden somebody wants the gay boys run out of the neighborhood?"

She meant it as a casual remark, but it set me to thinking.

I said, "The owner of Polly's had been tipped off that something was going to happen. But he didn't take the warning seriously."

"What was he going to do? Shut the place down and spend August at the seashore?"

"Miller figured it'd be a while before there'd be another raid, and he probably thought it would be an entirely different neighborhood, due for some commotion."

"Well, Nelson's not in bed with the mob. The same with Stem, no gangland ties, as far as we know. The other thing they have in common is their location. Could there be something to that?"

The breathy call of a train whistle wafted through the soggy night air. We were standing just four blocks from my office. The Pennsy's Chinese wall loomed up behind Polly-Wolly's.

"I guess it's possible," I said, "that mob guys—maybe the Russos— want to take over the two gay bars in this part of town, and they're using the cops to soften up the current proprietors. But if so, they'd have to cut other people in, like The Hat. Wise guys generally don't like to share. Anyway, they have their more subtle methods, like saying Hi, nice little saloon you got here, we sure hope it never goes up in a twelve-alarm blaze."

"Dyke bars don't have these problems," Mary Ann said with a tight smile. "They're all owned by criminals. Male criminals. It's just the natural order of things."

I told her about the German a hundred years ago who Amos Leary had said wanted to subvert the natural order by doing away with sodomy laws.

Mary Ann laughed. "Well, good for that guy. Did he end up in the loony bin?"

"Or the pokey."

Two cops came out of the bar. They had handcuffed a man and were leading him toward the squad car. He had a white cloth wrapped around his head that was red with what I guessed was blood. He staggered a bit before one of the officers shoved him into the back seat of the cruiser.

"Jesus," Mary Ann said. "What in God's name did they do to him? That's Nelson Miller."

CHAPTER 7

Back at my place, I took another shower. Then I half filled a clean pimento sandwich-spread jar with a fluid of a reassuring color, lit a cigarette, and phoned Byron Summerson. I hoped he would still be up at getting close to midnight. He was.

"I appreciated your calling me," I told him. "I went over to Polly's in time to see the owner getting dragged away by some officers. Adding injury to insult, it looked like they had roughed him up pretty badly. It's loony tunes what's going on, but I really have no idea what the hell it is."

"I just came up the hill from Leslie's quarters," Summerson said, "and he's becoming increasingly anxious. He was notified by Gary Trask that his court date will be Monday, and he told me that when he received this notification the poor soul burst into tears. We hope and pray, Mr. Waterman, that you will have come up with some type of solution for Leslie's situation by that date, if not, preferably, much sooner. Are you able to report any progress at all?"

"Byron, it's only been half a day, for chrissakes. I'm an investigator, not Mandrake the Magician. Tomorrow I'm going to try to get to somebody who's close to Ray Phipps, and I'll try to find out if there's a way to fix this thing. Or at least fix it for less than five hundred."

There was a silence, and then he enunciated a reply. "Well, if not that enormous sum, then what other amount might we have to come up with? Surely not more than perhaps a hundred dollars. I could perhaps borrow that much."

"I grew up believing," I said, "that out in Chestnut Hill money grew on trees. I guess I was wrong."

I could hear him sigh. "Once upon a time that was the case."

"You can't put on a bake sale or something? A tea?"

"Few people either I or Leslie know will want to have their names and reputations associated with anything so sordid as this set of circumstances. He has friends in the amateur theater group he's in who wish him well, but these are not people with much in the way of liquid assets. That's the reason I have taken the advice of Leslie's attorney and brought you into the picture. I thought that surely you would have understood that."

Meeting acquaintances for a brew or two, and with luck maybe a little hoochie-coochie later on, and getting arrested for it—that's what was "sordid."

I said, "Look, Byron, your friend is not alone in this and it all smells to high heaven. Others I know of are getting squeezed. Earlier tonight I talked to one of the Stem-raid victims who had to sell his car to pay off The Hat and his gang of extortionists. All I'm saying is: this thing is very big—bigger than you or your friend and certainly bigger than a dishonorably discharged small-beer queer shamus such as myself."

"Are you saying you can't help us?"

"No, I am going to do what I can do, and I'll try to not let you down, but I'm just being honest about the situation and telling you that we're going to have to see how it shakes out."

Summerson grew quiet again. Then: "I don't own a car I can sell. Nor does Leslie. We use public transportation. It's the reason why I was obliged to walk through that disgusting tunnel under the railroad in order to reach your office today."

"I apologize for that."

"My present fashionable address means nothing. Nothing whatsoever. You may not be aware that much of the Chestnut Hill wealth vanished under Herbert Hoover, and the socialist Roosevelt confiscated quite a lot of the rest."

"Yeah, word of all that did reach North Philly."

"It's probably just going to make you laugh, Mr. Waterman, but by the end of the last decade, my parents were complaining because they had been forced to play golf on a public golf course."

"Well, that is kind of funny."

"I am glad you phoned me. Otherwise I would have phoned you first thing in the morning. I told Leslie you seemed both competent and determined, and he would like very much to meet you. I may be wrong, but I am guessing he will find your somewhat rough-hewn manner to be just what is needed in a situation as fraught as the one he finds himself in. His spirits might be buoyed, and that seems urgent at the present moment."

"Okay, sure."

"Tomorrow? Say, late in the day? Perhaps we could all dine together at some modest *boîte*. And one would hope you might even have some good or at least promising news to relate during the get-together."

I agreed and suggested we meet at seven at Ted's, below my office. That fit the word modest if any place did. But Summerson was filled with horror at the idea of having to make his way under the Chinese wall again, so we settled on a place near Rittenhouse Square I knew they could easily reach by bus.

We hung up and I slugged down the remainder of my amber fluid. It seemed like I'd earned the right to a hot and fitful night's rest, but no such luck. The phone rang again. *Summerson calling back?*

"Yeah?"

"Clifford Waterman?"

"Yeah."

"I apologize for calling at this ridiculous hour, but I'm in a kind of bad situation—or my roommate is. An acquaintance of mine said he heard you are investigating the bar raid situation, and this situation seems to have something to do with that."

The caller gave me his name, Trevor Dunlap, and I asked him what the problem was.

"My roommate, Tom Heimer, was arrested at Stem t' Stern on Monday night. He has a court date on Monday, and now he seems to have disappeared."

CHAPTER 8

So now I had two clients. That made it interesting, though not lucrative, as Trevor Dunlap said that he also was a bit short. He seemed to want to piggyback on the Byron Summerson account, but I said nuh-uh to that.

I slept poorly in the hot bedroom; where was my Arab boy with a palm frond? I got out of bed just after three to take a piss and then—why not?—enjoy a smoke. It was quiet down on the street, except for a fire truck wailing for a few seconds in the distance. A gay bar fire?

I knew Tom Heimer, the missing roommate, a little. He'd had a fling with Monnie Hinkle, and so had I not long after I got back from the army. Montrose Hinkle Jr. was a Negro jazz saxophonist who worked with colored Philly dance bands for cash but liked to take the train up to New York when he could and play this new thing called bebop. Monnie once played a record of it for me. This was jazz that sounded a lot like a nervous breakdown, but I could tell I might get to like it.

Heimer and Trevor Dunlap were not boyfriends but shared an apartment over near Pennsylvania Hospital to save money. Dunlap told me Heimer was worried about losing his job as a high school industrial arts teacher, but he had no way of coming up with the five hundred for The Hat. He'd been emotionally distraught ever since the raid on Monday, and then today he hadn't come home after school and hadn't called to say where he was.

I told Dunlap it's police policy to wait twenty-four hours before you can report someone as a missing person. He said his roommate had always let him know if he'd be away overnight—shacking up or whatever—and this time there'd been no word, so something was definitely wrong.

When the alarm went off at seven, I wanted to throw the thing out the window. Instead, I shut it off and rewound it. I had a nickname for my alarm clock the way some people have nicknames for their cars, and it was Sisyphus.

I phoned the guy I knew who had a line into Ray Phipps and The Hat. When I was with the police I had once done him a favor in a jam involving his teenaged son. The kid had drunk to excess while behind the wheel and had had a loud encounter with a roadside kennel full of Pekingese puppies. Now the kid's dad always took my calls, and he invited me out to his house in Broomall for lunch.

I approached my office around eight-thirty, and as I maneuvered my way under the filthy PRR granite viaduct, the Chinese wall, I experienced the moldy cavern leading to the wall's north side through Byron Summerson's innocent blue eyes. He was right; the disgusting tunnel leaked God-knows-what from up above and stank of piss and garbage. On the sidewalk, where the cracks could break your mother's back, you had to walk around a rusted tricycle missing its big front wheel. Maybe some ladies club from Chestnut Hill that Summerson knew would come down to the tunnel and pick it up.

I grabbed coffee and a donut at Ted's and was at my desk finishing up a call with Summerson—he had nothing new to report—when Trevor Dunlap came in. He said he'd called the US Mint to say he'd be late for work but couldn't stay long without getting his pay docked. A short, wiry guy of sixty or so with a thinning gray pompadour, Dunlap was nicely turned out in the federal employee manner and wasn't sweating much yet. His tie had little dollar signs running up and down it, and I was betting it was a Christmas gift from a relative.

He said there was still no word from Tom Heimer, nor had their mutual friends he'd phoned heard from him.

"Monnie Hinkle told me," Dunlap said, "that Tom called him on Tuesday and was pretty upset over getting arrested and what all was going to happen, and could he come over and see Monnie Tuesday night? Monnie wasn't crazy about the idea. I think he thinks Tom is kind of a pain in the ass, pardon my pun."

"Mm."

"Those two were an item for a couple of months a few years ago. You probably know that Tom goes for the dark meat."

"Apparently so."

"Monnie must have gotten tired of Tom. The guy can be clingy. He comes on too strong sometimes. With his far-left political opinions but also the personal stuff. It took a while for Tom to accept the fact that this thing they had going just wasn't going to work out. Eventually he gave up. Tom was mixed up for a while with another gentleman of the colored persuasion, but that didn't go anywhere either—a shoeshine boy at Thirtieth Street Station."

"Uh huh."

"Then on Tuesday Monnie gets this call from Tom out of the blue. Monnie said Tom was in a panic because of the arrest, and if he got his name in the paper as a fag he'd probably lose his teaching job. Monnie said he agreed to meet Tom that night at eight at Maxine's. You know Maxine's I take it."

"I do."

"Piss elegant."

"You have to make sure you've applied the correct hair tonic and your necktie doesn't have any clam sauce stains on it."

"Except Tom never showed up. He came back to the

apartment late after wherever he'd been and went to bed. Then he got up yesterday and went to work, supposedly. Except that's the last anybody saw of him. He never showed up at school and never called in. Also, a guy from the teacher's union phoned, and Tom wasn't at their meeting last night, which was a problem because he's the treasurer."

"Oh?"

"Tom is true blue labor. I won't be surprised if he votes for Truman or even Henry Wallace."

"When you say, Mr. Dunlap, that Tom is the union treasurer, does that mean, for instance, that he has hold of the local's checkbook?"

Dunlap went through the motions of looking as if what I was thinking had never occurred to him. "I suppose he would have possession of the checkbook and access to the local organization's funds."

Would a union local have five hundred dollars in its checking account? I guessed it probably would.

I didn't like Trevor Dunlap at all, and I didn't like where this particular item of the Stem t' Stern raid fallout might be leading. But I accepted ninety dollars—four twenties and a ten—from Trevor Dunlap and stuffed it in my left front pocket.

CHAPTER 9

As soon as Dunlap left I phoned Monnie Hinkle. He was just getting in and was about to fall into bed at a little before 10 a.m. When he told me not to trust anything Trevor Dunlap said, I thought *uh-oh* and made a plan to meet Monnie that night to learn more. Then I got ready for my lunch date.

The Plymouth didn't like hot weather. It had a slow radiator leak, and I kept a watering can behind the driver's seat. I used it before I set out for Broomall, then refilled the can at the spigot by Ted's back door.

Driving out to Broomall, I checked WCAU for any news of the Polly-Wolly raid, but there wasn't any, an episode not worth mentioning. It was just a man shot his wife in a store over in Jersey, unions were going to have to start filing anti-Red oaths, and the Phils were having a lousy week. I switched to a station playing Ted Weems's "Heartaches," which was fitting because the Plymouth acted as if it liked rhumbas, even if maybe it only needed a front-end wheel alignment.

I hadn't been to Mike Stover's house since the sad episode with the small excitable dogs, but it hadn't changed. There were a couple of acres of rolling lawn reaching up to a sprawling edifice made of enough blocks of Pennsylvania schist to empty a quarry, with some important elm trees on either side of the main entrance that were probably planted by William Penn. I parked and walked up to a white front door that had two little peekaboo windows up high. I turned what looked like a brass faucet handle. The thing that sounded inside could have been the ringer on Bell's first phone: *Watson, come here, I want you.*

Stover appeared in less than a minute. His smile had a note of apology in it, the way it had seven years earlier, but otherwise his manner was that of a man who felt safe in his life's station. Which was deputy county chairman of his political party and owner of a chain of tire stores that dominated the market from Wilmington to Scranton. I remembered that the Plymouth could use a new left rear. Could I get a deal?

Stover was also a well-known supporter of good causes, charitable and artistic, and had enough civic awards to get him into Presbyterian heaven and maybe Episcopalian, too. His wife was once pictured in the *Inquirer* being handed a silver-looking scepter by the King of Denmark.

Around my size, middle-weight, but maybe ten years older, Stover was in what looked like a golfing outfit—*was there a putting green or even an eighteen-hole course on the property?*—and that was probably why his chiseled jaw and noble brow were healthily tanned with only a hint of overexposure to Old Sol.

I followed him through his cool, dark abode to a French door leading to a terrace with a yellow canvas canopy over some of it. There were enough wrought iron tables and cushioned chairs to handle Howard Hughes and his entourage if they happened by, and Ava Gardner, too. After I'd been led to a seat that looked out over more lawn and a small cherry orchard with a gazebo next to it, Stover poured me a bourbon. He was drinking a German beer he told me was now brewed in Argentina, and I wondered about that.

"I see you got through the war unscathed," Stover said, and then, remembering something he had no doubt recently been informed of, corrected himself. "Well, maybe not unscathed but anyway with no visible scars."

"I was lucky," I said, "in the most important ways." I told him about my two years in Cairo, without mentioning Idriss.

"I was sorry to hear," he said, "that you weren't able to resume your career as a police detective. I'll bet by now you'd be a senior officer on the force. I recall that you had a good grasp of the most modern principles of law enforcement while still bringing a high degree of common sense to the tasks at hand."

"Yeah, I was planning to go back."

"I'd try to help you out, but . . . well, for one thing, wrong county."

Somebody had left a big platter of sandwiches on the table, and I helped myself to a few. They were small sandwiches with cream cheese and bits of a green plant. The crusts had been cut off all the sandwiches. I guessed there were a lot of happy birds flying around Broomall.

I told Stover there wasn't anything anybody could do about a dishonorable discharge from the army, and anyway I was making do.

"I heard that's what happened to you," Stover said, "and I'm sorry. I had a nephew who was like you sexually, and in a way I wish the army had found out and sent him home the way they did you. My brother would be ashamed, but I told him flat out that at least James would be alive. He agreed, though I'm sorry to say only reluctantly."

"Yeah, well. Where did your nephew die?"

"Normandy. On D-Day."

"Hell. Well, he didn't see a lot of combat."

"About ten minutes was all."

I wanted to know more about the unlucky James, who apparently was out of the closet with his family. Either that or they had made inquiries as to why young James did not have a female sweetheart with his photo on her dresser back in PA or wherever they lived, and somebody had ratted him out.

I was anxious to get to the point, but first I wanted clarification on a peripherally related matter. I asked Stover, "And your son Freddie came through the war okay, I hope?"

"He did. Fred was attached to an engineering company that did bridge building and repair behind the combat forces. His engineering degree from Lehigh was something he struggled with at the time, but it may have saved his life. To Lehigh University," Stover said, and we both raised a glass.

I transferred a couple more of the little sandwiches to my plate—my ground-floor luncheon purveyor Ted would have laughed at them—and then I got to the point. I told Stover I was glad he was okay with men being homosexual, because that was why I had come to see him. I described the way gay guys in Philly were routinely blackmailed and extorted not by criminals, but by the police, bail bondsmen, crooked lawyers, court officials, and even, in at least one notorious case, by a judge.

Stover listened to all this without saying a word. I was sure he already knew all about it. The guy was wired and he wasn't stupid. His expression didn't change much until I got to the current situation. I told him how in the past week or so the price for having a charge erased from court records had shot up from an outrageous but usually bearable fifty dollars to an impossible-for-many-people five hundred. I said one client of mine had been socked with this demand and couldn't pay it and feared for his job, and another client caught in this reprehensible trap had simply disappeared.

Stover's face tightened, and in his eyes I could see perplexity alternating with anger. I asked his advice on how the overall situation might be dealt with. Could, for example, the feds be brought in? And then I asked Stover specifically: could he get to somebody he knew and have Leslie Croyer's extortion fee kicked back down to fifty dollars?

I waited while Stover sipped his German/Argentinian

beer. For about a minute he said nothing at all. I had another sandwich.

"The thing is," Stover finally said, looking sour, "with the feds, forget it."

"Extortion's a crime," I said. "There must be some federal statute on that."

"I don't know if there is. I'd guess it's strictly a matter covered by the state criminal code. But even if there is a federal law, do you think J. Edgar Hoover is going to give a shit about any of this? If Judge Stetson was a communist when he was in junior high school, then we could talk about that. But I doubt if he was. In fact, you can be certain he wasn't. If he had been, you can bet the House Un-American Activities Committee would have hauled his ass in to testify months ago."

"The guy's a fucking gangster. A judge!"

"Hoover isn't interested in gangsters either, in case you haven't heard. Unless they have union connections."

I read the paper and knew everything Stover was telling me was true about Hoover and the feds, and I was wasting my time barking up that tree.

Bluntness was called for. "How about just getting some relief for this nice young guy, Leslie Croyer? His hearing is Monday with The Hat. Croyer's not out with his family or his employer, and he's practically suicidal. Help me out with his case, Mr. Stover. I am betting you can."

Stover's suntanned face was looking more animated now. Not quite twitchy, but its repose was gone for the moment. Finally, he said, "I do have friends who can sometimes help a person out who's been royally fucked by the system."

"I know. And here I am."

"But . . . Stetson and his people are . . . I don't know."

"Help me out here, sir. This is nothing to them, a speck of dandruff. The Stetson machine can afford to let one lousy queer be on his way."

"Of course they can, if they choose to."

"Will you help me out with this?" I thought about making Pekingese noises, *yap yap*.

For a long moment he fooled around with his glass of Argentinian beer—a product of the Josef Mengele Brewing Company?—and then he said, "Let me make a few calls. What if I get back to you later this afternoon, Clifford?"

"I'll be in my office."

There was a puddle under the Plymouth, but I had brought my watering can and filled it from Stover's hose with a tire wholesaler's water.

CHAPTER 10

Before I left, I asked Stover if he could also maybe get a better deal for Tom Heimer, the shop teacher who had gone missing. Stover said he'd have to see. Who knew? Maybe I could give him a list of everybody victimized in both the Stem t' Stern and Polly-Wolly raids and this sachem of the confederacy of Southeastern Pennsylvania political tribes could work some kind of voodoo, and all those unlucky guys could breathe easier. I wasn't getting my hopes up, though.

I was back in my office by a quarter of three. The heat hadn't let up and my fan was still dead to the world. A fly had gotten stuck on one of its blades and was struggling to free itself. I removed the screen from my window, pried the fly loose from the fan with a letter opener, and flicked the insect out into the void. It plummeted down toward Ted's back door as the Pennsy 1:55 from Washington Union Station screeched by an hour late.

I phoned Polly-Wolly's and got no answer and then called Sal Romeo who owned Sal's, a bar I liked. I asked him if he knew anything about Nelson Miller, Polly-Wolly's owner who'd been arrested and knocked around the night before.

"He made bail," Sal said, "but then it looked like maybe he had a concussion, so I heard Nelson is in Jefferson, or maybe Philly. Hey, what the fuck is going on with all this bullshit cop stuff all of a sudden? You got any idea, Cliff?"

"I'm trying to find out."

"I mean, two in one week? What the goddamn fuck?"

"It's excessive, that's for sure."

"The vice squad is also out of control. I heard of three entrapments yesterday alone—that little tearoom over by Broad Street Station. A guy comes on to a second guy, and then the first guy whips out the cuffs. It's like they got some kind of homo assembly line going on over at The Hat's courthouse."

"I know. I'm trying to help two guys out."

"My business is down. People aren't going out. It stinks, and nobody knows what the fuck all this is."

"I'm waiting for a call now. I might know more later."

"I mean, what the hell are we supposed to do?"

"That's the question, all right."

Across the room the mail slot clunked open, and some envelopes sailed through the opening.

I told Sal I'd let him know if I heard anything new and he said he'd do the same.

The mail was of no use or interest except for one thing: Bell Telephone of Pennsylvania was notifying me it would cut off my office phone unless I coughed up fourteen dollars by the twenty-seventh, next Wednesday. *Watson, come here, and bring your wallet.*

I tried to reach Bobby Carletti to find out if he'd picked up any dope on all the gay bar raids going on all of a sudden, but he was on duty and out of reach for civilians. So I sat by the phone and waited for Mike Stover to call. I tugged up a 7Up from Ted's. I was tempted to order up a growler—Stover's dainty sandwiches not having done the job—but I would be dining in a few hours with Byron Summerson and Leslie Croyer, so I restrained myself. I did have one little nip from the desk drawer and with it a Lucky. *L-S-M-F-T —Lucky Strike Means Fine Tobacco*, truer words never having been spoken.

His word being his bond, Mike Stover phoned me a little after four.

"I'm so sorry, Clifford, that my news is not all that good."

Not all that—did that leave room for hope?

"Ah-ha. So, what's the word?"

"As we both suspected, what we're dealing with here is a group of people who are impervious to reason."

"Impervious."

"It's not just that they are hard-nosed, which they very much are, but there seems to be something underway at the present moment that has made this—what's the word I want? *consortium?*—particularly intransigent."

"A bunch of pricks."

"They're not only unyielding, they aren't even approachable."

"That's unfortunate."

"Normally, I can provide at least a degree of assistance in certain complex situations, but there's an aggressiveness here that's without precedent in my experience, Clifford."

"And you've had a lot of experience."

"But this one has me flummoxed."

"So, what's the deal, Mike? You can't even help out with the Leslie Croyer situation? I mean, it is such a small, small, small thing, really."

"God, I so wish I could. I want you to know, I tried."

I looked out the window at another coal eater hissing by.

"Is there anyone else you know I can call? Give me a name and a number, Mike. Maybe if I make a direct appeal to somebody whose heart is not totally hardened, it will make a difference."

I was pleading by now, but I knew I was just emitting gasses like the big dumb machine that had just passed by my window, except that the steam engine was getting somewhere and I wasn't.

"I'll tell you what I can do, Clifford, to help out your friend

Leslie. I'd like to contribute fifty dollars. Maybe that will prime the pump, and I'm sure you have other acquaintances. Or even perhaps additional persons such as myself whom you assisted in a discreet manner when you were back on the force in Philly. How can I get the amount to you? It will be in cash and there's no need to mention where it came from. Just say it's from someone who holds no animus against homosexuals. In my mind, I will be making this donation in the memory of my nephew James, and it will make me happy to do it."

I told Stover how his courier could drop off the envelope with the fifty at Ted's Luncheonette and I'd pick it up there.

I hung up and sat staring at nothing much.

CHAPTER 11

Who else could I put the touch on? Back on the force, I had helped a few other people of means work through situations, and of course numerous not-so-well-off people also. I had not received or wanted anything in return. I believed at the time it was just a question of the law not being a total asshole.

I had joined the police after Dad had his stroke and we couldn't afford Millersville State anymore, even after Mom started work at Fanny Farmer's. Dad's brother Herb had been a cop, and it looked like a decent enough way to make your way across this mortal coil. The pay was okay and you never got fired. At the time, Uncle Herb told me, "You can get up in the morning and know you're going to help out people who deserve it, and you can push around people who deserve that." Being young, I thought, *who could argue with such a point of view?* Naturally, it all turned out to be more complicated.

I thought of two upper-crust people I might call informally. I'd helped them out of a tough spot, but I wasn't even sure how to get in touch with them. And the chances were good they would tell me to fuck off or try to notify my superiors, not knowing I had been let loose from the police on account of an indecent act with a native.

I thought about dropping by the courthouse and either

pleading with Ray Phipps or threatening him. But if Mike Stover or any of his people had asked nicely and come up with "nuh uh," how was I going to make out any better? And the only way I knew to threaten Phipps was to tell him I was going to expose him as a criminal, and he'd die laughing over that. Of course, I could threaten Phipps physically, but then I'd land in the lockup myself until I could produce my own five hundred. If you're going to overthrow the king, you have to cut his head off. Maybe pick up my .38 and shoot Ray Phipps through the heart and then blast The Hat too? It was tempting, and they both had it coming.

Instead, I pulled out my bottom drawer, had a small pick-me-up along with my pop, and lit another cigarette.

The phone rang. It was Bobby Carletti calling on his meal break.

"I just had to let you know," he said, "that your name has come up."

"In what regard?"

"In regards to you might have wandered into some deep shit that it would be wise to back up and step out of."

"What deep shit? You mean, trying to keep a couple of sociable queers from being bankrupted by a bunch of gangsters at the courthouse?"

"Are you working on anything else?"

"No."

"Then that's it."

"I'm puzzled. Who even knows what I'm doing?" I asked, making a list in my head.

"Well, somebody," Carletti said. "There's some major crapola that's going on, and the word in the department is to come down on homos, and that has something to do with this larger thing. You've been showing signs of possibly being a hindrance."

"What the hell? There's no election this year. I don't get it. Unless—is it the archdiocese?"

"I told you all I know, Clifford. Protect yourself. There are people in the department who remember you. Some of them would be sorry if anything bad happened to you, but some of them would stamp and cheer. You probably know that."

"Can you get me a list?"

"A list of what? I gave you a list."

"Never mind."

"I gotta get back to my shift. I'm suggesting that maybe you should back away from this situation, whatever it turns out to be, and do it fast and do it in a way everybody can take notice of."

"I appreciate the advice, Bobby, but we'll have to see."

"I wouldn't want you to get a busted lip. Nobody wants to kiss one of them."

I remembered how years ago I'd been in a bar fight involving eight or ten guys, and afterward I'd gone home with one of the participants. We both were pretty banged up, and our enthusiastic not-so-quasi-erotic behavior required a certain amount of ingenuity, proving where there's a will, there's a way.

I told Bobby, "I'll keep an eye out for whatever or whoever might want to play rough. Should I be carrying a weapon? I don't want to be caught either unawares or unprepared."

After a moment, he said, "It sounds to me, Clifford, like doing something like that would just be asking for trouble. Why the hell don't you just find something entirely different to do? Jesus, just try to be a little practical for a change. I mean—I know I can be totally up front with you. Try what I would call living in the real world, and, knowing you as I do, I think you would call it that, too."

I told Bobby I appreciated the Dutch uncle advice. Then I hung up and sat for a long time wondering what was up with him. Who had had him call me, and why?

CHAPTER 12

I still had time to kill before going over to meet Byron Summerson and Leslie Croyer for our supper near the square. So I started working my other case and tried phoning the names Trevor Dunlap had given me. Supposedly these were friends of Tom Heimer who might have an idea what had become of him. Probably because it was a Thursday afternoon and people were still at work, I got a lot of no answers. I did reach one person, a woman named Deidre Dunphy who Dunlap said was a retired teacher at the school where Heimer taught. She still substitute-taught there sometimes, and she was a chum of Heimer's.

She told me she was glad I was looking for Tom because she was starting to worry that something had happened to him.

"I ran into Tom in the teachers' room on Tuesday morning," Dunphy said. "He was pretty upset about getting arrested, though he said he thought he had figured out a way to deal with the situation without pleading guilty. So I was surprised when Trevor said he had apparently gone missing."

"Did he mention anything about paying officials off to have the charges dismissed?"

She coughed and I deduced she had dragged on a cigarette that was probably too strong for her.

"He didn't say what it was. Just that he wasn't going to let the arrest mess up his entire life. He was pretty agitated when he talked about the whole thing, but I would say he was more mad than frightened. Which isn't surprising, because Tom has a temper, though it's generally political things that set him off. Topics of social justice, he would call them. Of course, I guess his getting arrested just for being in a bar minding his own business would fit into that category."

"I think it would."

"If it was me, I'd have been scared silly. The Philadelphia School Department does not approve of its employees being hauled in by the police. Especially for disorderly conduct, so-called. That's what they call it if you're a homosexual. Or am I giving something away about Tom that I'm not supposed to? Uh oh."

"No, it's okay, I'm disorderly too."

"Oh. Well. A gay private eye! That's unusual. Well, good for you, Mr. Waterman."

"Yeah, I'm a novelty in my line of work. Or as far as I know I am."

"People have their ideas. But stereotypes can be misleading. For instance, my hairdresser, Raoul of Society Hill. He comes across as gay, but he's actually straight."

I knew Raoul. On occasion, we had trimmed each other's bangs. But there was no point in my mentioning this.

I said, "Tom didn't show up at school yesterday, and he didn't appear last night at his teacher's union meeting either. When you saw him on Tuesday, he didn't say anything about that?"

"Not to me. I know Tom is pro-union all the way. Like my late husband was before the war. Tom's even one of the officials."

"The treasurer, I was told."

"Yes, I guess I knew that."

She cleared her throat as if to speak but had nothing more to add on the topic of Heimer's apparently being in possession of the union local's checkbook.

"It's my understanding," I said, "that Trevor Dunlap called you asking what you might know about Tom's whereabouts. Is Trevor somebody you know well?"

"Not really. He's Tom's roommate, but I think that's only for convenience. Trevor works at the mint, and I have the impression that his social life revolves around other mint employees. A couple of us from school were having a Friday after-work drink one time, and Trevor and some other men in topcoats came in. Tom said, 'They're mint,' and he didn't seem to want to have anything to do with them. I know he would prefer to live alone if he could afford it."

I understood that United States Mint people tended to keep mum about their work producing the nation's currency and they often hung out together. Not a weird cult or anything, but a little bit of a snoot-in-the-air fraternity.

I asked, "But Trevor is gay, too, isn't he? Or maybe you don't know."

She hesitated. "I think so, but I'm not sure," she replied, a little uneasily, probably thinking, *Why is this guy asking me something like that?*

I'd have to wait until I saw Monnie Hinkle later that evening to get more dope on Trevor. Monnie had said Trevor was not to be trusted, and what was that about? Without mentioning Monnie, I asked Dunphy if she knew of any current or former boyfriends Tom had who I should check with.

"Tom has always been rather private about his romantic life," she said. "So I really wouldn't know. There was a colored fellow, a large man with a beard, I know, that I saw Tom with a couple of times, and I thought they might be on a date. But maybe not. I can tell you that *that* would not have gone over well in the teachers' lounge."

It was soon plain that Dunphy had no additional information that was useful or even interesting to either of us. She said she would call me if she heard from Heimer or if she thought of anything that might be helpful. I said I'd ask Heimer to call her if and when I located him.

After I hung up, I only had time to look out and wave at the folks pulling into Broad Street Station from Baltimore before the phone rang again.

"Your line's been busy." The male voice was thin and croaky.

"Yes, it has."

"I tried earlier too."

"I was out of the office on a professional matter."

"You don't know who this is, do you?"

"No, I don't. Why don't you inform me?"

"My esophagus is bruised or some shit. And I have a concussion. It's me, Clifford, Nelson Miller."

"Jesus. Nelson. Those officers really worked you over. I was there when they shoved you in the squad car, all bloody and practically falling over. Are you going to be all right?"

"In a week or so, they say. Right now I feel awful, like I got run over."

"Yeah, well, you did. By the PPD."

"I'm in Jefferson."

"They'll take good care of you."

He coughed. Surely they weren't letting him smoke.

"Those goddamn cops didn't have to beat me up, you know. I didn't do anything to provoke them."

"I wondered about that."

"Polly's has gotten raided before. About twice a year, in fact. And I just cooperate and pay the baksheesh to the courthouse blackmailers, and then life moves on. You don't like it, but you kind of get used to it. Queer *c'est la vie*."

"I know."

"But this time was different."

"More violent, you mean?"

"That, and something else. Something the captain who seemed to be in charge said to me after we got to the precinct."

"What was that?"

"He said I was going to close down my business."

"And you weren't planning to?"

"No." Miller's voice was getting raspier, and I wondered if he shouldn't be giving his esophagus a rest. But what was going on here?

"But that's illogical. You close down and all the courthouse extortionists will lose business."

"I know. I don't get it. The building I'm in has a new owner, some real estate guy. When he bought the place in May, he said I had to vacate by the end of August, and I said I didn't have to on account of I have a lease that runs three more years. The guy backed off, but now I'm wondering if this thing and what the precinct captain said aren't connected."

"It sounds like they might be."

Miller's voice had started to fade away, but now he cleared his throat, and this was followed by a little cry of pain.

"I had to call you," he managed to say, "because I heard you were investigating whatever the fuck is going on here."

I said I was.

"And I thought I had to tell you that you really should leave this whole goddamned mess alone."

"Uh huh."

"A cop I know warned me something bad was going to happen, and I didn't listen."

"You said."

"But this guy called me here in my hospital bed this afternoon, and this sympathetic officer—he is in the know at PPD, I can guarantee you that—and this officer said anybody who keeps pushing against this thing is going to get badly injured. Even a lot worse than me, he said. And I believe him."

"Hell."

"Even those poor bastards who were just having a convivial social occasion, and got nailed for disturbing the peace. He said they have to cooperate—pay the fine, or go to jail, or fork over whatever they're charged by Ray Phipps and The Hat, or they're going to get hurt. Like me. I heard you were trying to help out some of the victims of the raid and the one at Stem. Take my word and don't do it. Just tell your clients to do as they are told or be prepared to suffer the consequences."

"Jesus."

"Will you just pass that on, Cliff?"

I told Miller I appreciated his information and his insights, and I promised him I would certainly mull over how he had advised me to proceed. Then I sat for some minutes doing just that. This is what I came up with: I'd been warned off the investigation by Bobby, and now Miller had passed along the same warning from a source in the PPD. Anybody with one-tenth of a brain would have taken their advice.

CHAPTER 13

Mom's sister Thelma's husband, Grant—who, not having served in the military, still insisted the guys in his department at the plant where he worked call him General Grant—liked to spout so-called words of wisdom like he'd invented them. One of his favorites was, "You can't fight city hall." But I had taken a couple of American history courses at Millersville while I was still there and had learned that fighting city hall was as American as rhubarb pie, and if you kept at it you might win. Look at the labor movement. You might also end up with all your teeth flying out the front of your face, but not necessarily.

On the other hand—here was another General Grantism—you had to pick your battles. I learned the truth of that both in the police and in the army. While I did not want to get my esophagus bruised or my brain rattling around the inside of my skull at the hands of members of the PDD like what had happened to Miller, I also did not want any of that to happen to Leslie Croyer. Or Tom Heimer, or Amos Leary, or anybody else caught up in the recent bar raids. So, what to advise Croyer and my client Byron Summerson?

They were already seated next to each other in a booth at Burkett's Fine Dining when I got there a little before seven. My expectation was that Croyer would be a fragile fellow, but he sure didn't look the part. A good six-two, muscular, with floppy brown hair above a Joe Palooka face that was easy to look at, Croyer could have passed for a guy in a shaving cream ad. He was in tan slacks and a green shirt unbuttoned to show a smidgen of broad chest cleavage.

Seated against the wall, Summerson was fidgeting with a glass of ice water as I sat down facing them. The restaurant was crowded and noisy, so we all spoke up for the introductions. Luckily, the air-conditioning was working, though that added to the racket. I was ready to chow down after my inadequate luncheon of Mrs. Tremblechin's bitsy sandwiches. And I still hadn't decided what exactly I was going to tell the aggrieved victim of The Hat and the good-hearted fussbudget who was in love with him and wanted to help him out. Famished though I was, I understood why the two men wanted to get to the point. So I put off examining the menu, which anyway I pretty much knew by heart.

"If I may so inquire, what is your report?" Summerson asked. "You had a helpful contact, you said. Were you able to strike a deal?"

"I'm afraid not," I said, and their faces fell. "The thing is, what we have here is an abnormal situation. Whatever's going on is so unusual there's none of the usual predictable response when you apply the normal stimuli."

They both stared at me.

"What I mean is, there are two systems of justice, all right? There's the one in the Constitution and in the laws the politicians wrote and that lawyers and judges were taught and that they normally employ. Then there's the other justice system, the unwritten one, that's more behind-the-scenes—if you know what I mean—and it works sometimes for the better and sometimes for the worse."

They sat waiting for any point I might eventually get around to making.

"Right now, in Philly," I said, "neither justice system is functioning properly. Well, the official justice system has never worked for us, but sometimes an unofficial one could, with a little greasing of the wheels. But things have gone haywire. I was reliably informed this afternoon that Judge Stetson and Ray Phipps, the judge's detestable bagman, are at the moment . . . *impervious to reason* was how it was put to me. Normally they have always been hard-nosed. Especially when it came to homosexuals, as is well known, but now they're out of control."

They flinched, almost in unison, and Summerson did a quick look-see at the booths nearby to try to make out if anybody had overheard my controversial terminology. Croyer sat rigid and fixed his gaze on the ridge of my nose.

"I did learn," I went on, "that whatever the degree of injustice being perpetrated against"—I was more careful now—"certain types of people in the city, now is probably not a good time to challenge the unfortunate status quo. You'll be inclined to ask, then when would be a good time? I'm afraid the answer is, I don't know."

I could see them sitting there concluding that I was a useless bullshit artist and that Summerson should ask for his money back.

"So then, what am I supposed to do?" Croyer asked. He had a resonant voice, like a singer or an announcer on the radio, but now it was coming out shaky. "I don't really understand what you're saying, Mr. Waterman."

"I think," I said, "that unless you have another route to getting this thing fixed—I mean a discount from the five hundred—you just have to figure out a way to pay it."

They looked newly aghast.

"I can help out a little in that regard," I said. "Since despite my strenuous endeavors I came up empty, Byron, I'll return your ninety dollars. Plus, a sympathetic interested party wants to donate, too. He gave me fifty to pass on to you. And since you said you could scare up a hundred, that leaves you with—what? Another three hundred and fifty or so to round up by Monday."

Croyer placed his face in his hands and shook. Summerson glared at me.

I said, "Leslie, Byron tells me you're from upstate. I know you're not out of the closet with your family, and I understand how that can be a huge problem. But couldn't you just call them and tell them an emergency has come up, and ask if you can borrow some money? And then just—well, make up some story?"

Now Croyer was quietly weeping, and Summerson was alternately glancing around at the other diners and shooting eye daggers at my carotid.

I didn't know what to say or do. Picking up the menu would only worsen the situation. I peered down at the paper placemat in front of me. It featured drawings of famous Philadelphia sights and scenes: Independence Hall, Betsy Ross's house, bespectacled Ben Franklin flying a kite in a thunderstorm. As I recalled, old Ben had offspring, and I wondered what his kids made of that habit of his.

I wondered, should I tell them that if they didn't find a way to satisfy The Hat's regime they might actually be in physical danger? I wasn't sure I entirely bought into the warnings from Bobby Carletti and Nelson Miller, but there was plenty of evidence that something desperate was going on and these two might somehow be at risk.

I said, "Or what if you just plead guilty, Leslie, and pay the disturbing the peace fine, and hope the *Inquirer* doesn't put your name in the paper? Sometimes they don't. Like if there's a lot of other news that day. Like if the Phils' shortstop is stopped for a DUI or something."

This was lame and got the reaction it deserved. Croyer uncovered his face and spat out at me, "And what if Gertrude Lawrence came to Philly and went on stage at the Shubert and shit scrapple with maple syrup? *What if! What if!*"

Where'd that come from? Did people talk like that up in—which town was it? Lock Haven?

Following a few more uncomplimentary remarks concerning my professional competence, Croyer and Summerson got up and left. I gave Summerson his ninety back, plus the fifty Mike Stover had been kind enough to have dropped off at Ted's. I still had ninety from the mysterious—that's how I now thought of him—US Mint employee Trevor Dunlap. I perused the Burkett's Fine Dining menu, skipping over the scrapple.

CHAPTER 14

Montrose Hinkle Jr. came from a family of musicians. His dad was a music professor at a colored college near Baltimore, and his mom played the organ at church. They knew he was gay and had gotten used to it—his dad had a gay cousin in DC that the family liked—though Monnie had once told me that if his maternal grandmother ever saw Monnie with me she'd yell at him for having anything to do with a white devil.

We had met at a club on South Street that was mostly Negro and was straight downstairs and gay upstairs with an interesting amount of traffic back and forth between the two. I went there because I liked the music, both swing and honking blues. Everybody was better dressed than I was, but nobody criticized me to my face.

I had dated Monnie for a while after the army threw me out, and the war ended. His own discharge had been honorable after two years in a Negro band unit that never saw action. We hit it off pretty well, but he also had a colored boyfriend living in France, a piano player he visited whenever he could pay the plane or boat fare. I didn't like feeling jealous or disappointed whenever he went off, so things petered out after a while between us, though we stayed friendly and still hopped in the sack every now and again for old time's sake and because we liked to.

"How'd you get mixed up in this bullshit that's going on?" Monnie asked me when he came up to my apartment just after nine. "I know you always like getting in trouble of some kind, but The Hat and those courthouse criminals? I don't know about *that*."

He tasted of marijuana, a thing I had tried a couple of times, but I still preferred fluids. I explained that I had two paying clients who were friends of the victims of the raids, not mentioning that I had given one of the clients his money back because I had failed to be helpful in any way at all.

"Well, Trevor Dunlap I'd be careful of," Monie said. "He works at the mint in security supposedly, but the NAACP people I know think he's some kind of snoop for Hoover."

"Oh hell."

"I know when Tom was looking for a roommate to save money on rent, all of a sudden Trevor showed up out of nowhere. Tom thought, oh, works for the mint, the guy sounds copacetic. But then Trevor always seemed to be asking too many questions about Tom's union stuff, and Tom wondered why."

"Not just curiosity?"

"Names of people and what their positions were and what they did, and such like."

"Uh oh."

"They've got the FBI coming down on unions, so what was going on here, Tom wondered."

"Looking for Reds?"

"And Tom was a natural for people who had that way of thinking."

"He was?"

We were naked on top of the sheets on my bed. We each had a glass of my Jim Beam and were enjoying a smoke. I had a medium-sized leg thrown over one of Monnie's long ones. The atmospheric conditions were good that August night, so my radio was picking up the powerful New Orleans all-jazz station that you could get sometimes. It was playing Billie Holiday with

Lester Young and a group doing "Fine and Mellow." This was good. We were both sweaty but the bedroom fan was working, almost like a breeze at the shore, though not quite.

"Tom's a total lefty," Monnie said. "I pretty much went along with his politics, but sometimes all the political stuff got annoying. Not the union stuff, but stuff like race."

Monnie hardly ever talked about race, so what was this? "How come annoying?"

"He was always going on about W.E.B. DuBois and him being a communist and an anti-imperialist and how great he was."

"Who?" The name was familiar but only because it was in *Inquirer* articles I probably meant to get around to reading but instead read "Jersey Man Shoots Wife in Store."

Monnie explained about this hero of the colored people and his books and speeches and how the FBI hated him.

I said, "He sounds like a good person, but I don't know about him being a Red."

"The thing was, it got to be like whenever we were screwing it was like it was a three-way with Tom and me and W.E.B. DuBois. He liked to say whenever he was with me, he felt closer to DuBois. It was a big turn-on for Tom. I finally asked him to cut it out. I said, Tom, maybe you should suck off Albert Einstein. You could eat the atomic bomb. But he kept it up, and it got to be really boring."

I saw Monnie's point, but I understood Tom also. When I had sex with Monnie I felt closer to Coleman Hawkins or whoever it was on the radio I was so crazy about. Though to Monnie, his dick was just his dick.

I said, "I guess I see what you mean."

"Don't get me wrong—there was a lot I really liked about Tom. He was quite intelligent, and big, and handsome. And he had a nice piece of meat, which I always appreciate, present company included."

"Always good to hear."

"But after a while, I had had enough of the DuBois weird shit and some of his other odd ways of thinking, and I broke up with him. He'd still call me once in a blue moon and we'd yak about this and that. When he called me after he was arrested in the Stem raid, he was pretty shaken up and I was going to meet him at Maxine's Tuesday night and hear what happened. I have to admit, I was curious to hear the story of the raid."

"You've never been caught in one?"

"I've been fucked over by cops more times than I can count. But never in a gay bar. Maybe they're scared to do it in certain neighborhoods, I don't know."

"But Tom never showed up at Maxine's on Tuesday."

"I waited till around nine. I had a club sandwich and went home. Trevor called me the next day and asked if I might know where Tom was and said that he hadn't showed up at school."

"And still hasn't checked in with anybody, as far as I know."

"He was really upset about the whole Stem thing. He knew the school was just itching for a way to shit-can a union troublemaker, and getting arrested in a homo bar would probably be his ticket to landing on his ass in the gutter."

The radio played some more Billie and Lester, the sweet and sour lament "I'll Never Be the Same." We had the lights out, but the streetlight out on Locust shone in on us, on Monnie's big whiskery face and ample frame and on mine that was sizable too and not entirely pale. My dad said he had a Leni Lenape ancestor—Mom's sister Thelma liked to call him "that Indian in the Waterman woodpile"—and maybe that was why some of the Watermans were what Aunt Thelma called "dark-complected." Anyway, I liked the way my lighter body absorbed the light coming through the window and Monnie's black skin reflected it.

I told Monnie that a teacher at Tom's school had said Tom told her Tuesday morning that he thought he had a way of not being found guilty of "disturbing the peace"—or whatever the charge from the Stem raid was going to be—and asked, had Tom said anything about that to him?

"Not exactly that," he said. I'd lit a fresh cigarette, and he took it from me for a drag. "But, come to think of it, he did say he had an idea he might want to run by me. Though he also said something about how this was an idea I might not want to hear."

"Oh? Any idea what he might have meant by that?"

"Nope. He might have been just talking. Tom's a talker."

I took the cigarette back from him and asked him if he had any ideas about other people Heimer might have gotten in touch with. People he might turn to in a desperate situation, which this certainly was.

Monnie said there was an old high school buddy who lived over in Bucks County somewhere, but Monnie couldn't remember the guy's name. That struck us both as a cue to forget Tom Heimer's troubles for a little while, and ours too, and all the cares of the world. On came Billie and Lester again with an up-tempo "*Ooo-ooo-ooo*, What a Little Moonlight Can Do."

Or streetlight.

CHAPTER 15

The bad news about Leslie Croyer didn't reach me until mid-morning. When it did, it hit me like a land mine going off ten feet away, especially since the fine and mellow night with Monnie had temporarily carried me so far away from any courthouse heebie-jeebies or PPD nasty surprises.

Monnie and I had slept in until almost nine and then had coffee and some shredded wheat with milk that was about a week old but still usable. We were both the worse for wear owing to the Jim Beam. He had brought along his toothbrush, which he said helped after he used my Ipana, erasing what he called a "dead canary taste"—*how would he know what that tasted like?*—and our first nicotine hits of the day also helped get rid of the stale flavor of last night's liquid and other pick-me-ups.

Monnie had two weekend band gigs coming up, he told me, and then on Monday he was taking the train up to New York for the weekly bop jam session at Minton's. I could tell he wanted to play this new jazz style all the time, but it wasn't a way he could pay the bills. He said he thought the situation might improve next year when a new type of record was coming out, long-playing. You could get thirty minutes of music on each side instead of just three, so more people could get to appreciate bebop and maybe it would even catch on in Philly.

I asked him, "Will I have to get a new record player?"

"Yeah, but it'll be worth it."

"It sounds like a racket, Stromberg-Carlson and RCA."

"Wait and see. The sound will be a hundred percent better, too."

When the phone rang, I thought, *Oh damn*, but with The Hat's courthouse shit flying every which way I had no choice but to answer it.

"You're not in your office, Mr. Waterman," came Byron Summerson's snippy voice.

"That's right."

"I've been phoning there since eight, and the phone just rings and rings."

"Phones will do that."

"Gary Trask knew someone who had possession of your home number, and all I can say is, thank God for that."

"So what's up, Byron? Have you and Leslie had any luck rounding up any additional dough for the courthouse extortionists? I just want to reiterate how bad I felt last night saying I had let you down. It's such a crummy situation, as I said, like nothing gay Philadelphia has ever seen before. Besides that, I don't know what else to tell you."

There was a long silence, and soon I became aware that Summerson was weeping.

"Byron?"

Now the crying was more pronounced.

"Take your time," I said, feeling useless and stupid.

Then he managed to blurt out, "He's dead."

I didn't have to ask. "Who is dead?"

More snuffling. "Leslie. Dear, dear Leslie."

"Oh no."

More weeping.

"What happened?" I asked, and tried to fortify myself for the answer I knew was coming.

"He killed himself."

"Oh, Byron. Oh no."

"He jumped off the bridge."

Jesus. "Which one?"

"Delaware."

That indicated Croyer meant it. "Oh God."

"He must have taken the bus down to the river and then walked across the bridge toward Camden. Around midnight a motorist observed a man sitting on the railing of the bridge with his legs on the wrong side for safety's sake. When the motorist arrived at his destination in New Jersey, he phoned the police."

"Good for that guy."

"It's on the radio. Don't you own a radio?"

It was still tuned to New Orleans and switched off. "I just got out of bed." There was no need to tell Summerson that while the tortured young man he loved was violently ending his life by plunging a hundred feet into the churning vortexes of the Delaware River, I was dozing off in the arms of a man who had just filled me with contentment.

Monnie was watching me talk, and his look told me he got the gist of what had happened. He sat at the kitchen table and sipped his coffee.

"It was Gary Trask who phoned me at six-fifteen this morning," Summerson said. "I had informed Gary last night that Leslie was distraught and had left the estate, and asked should I notify the police? He estimated, correctly I'm sure, that the police would not have reacted with alacrity."

"Probably not."

"Mr. Trask heard on the news that the body of a young man had been discovered by a refinery worker along the shore at Marcus Hook, and he placed a phone call and learned of the young man's identity. Fortunately, Leslie's wallet had remained in his pocket."

"That was lucky. Erasing any doubt."

"Yes, it basically left no question. Although there is another matter that is required by law. Mr. Trask volunteered my services for the grim task of identifying Leslie's body. And I reluctantly agreed to do so."

Up until then I hadn't been quite sure why Summerson found it so urgent to notify me of this terrible development—he had basically fired me as an investigator the night before—but now the main purpose of his call was beginning to come clear.

"Yeah, I guess it makes sense for you to be the one. It'll be really hard, I'm sure."

"The thing of it is . . . Summerson forged ahead. "I do not believe I can face this alone. Nor do I own an automobile."

"I know."

"I wish to ask you, Mr. Waterman, if you would kindly accompany me as I carry out this ghastly responsibility. I'll be happy to give you the ninety dollars back."

I looked over at Monnie, who peered back at me over his cool jazz man's bushy black beard. I could see he understood that I was in for something complicated.

CHAPTER 16

When I stopped by the office—going over to pick up the Plymouth, which was parked by Ted's back door—and Trevor Dunlap phoned, it almost felt like a welcome distraction.

"You just caught me. I'm in and out. Any news of Tom Heimer? I talked to Monnie Hinkle, but he wasn't able to provide any information beyond what he already told you."

"You know, I tried phoning earlier," Dunlap said. "Isn't Friday a business day?"

"Not in North Africa."

"What?"

"Look, I don't have a secretary to answer the phone because the one time I had one she broke up with her girlfriend, and then she came up here and spent the night on the floor and drank all my Wild Turkey. So, what were you calling me about earlier, and what is it you're calling me about now?"

"You know, I paid you ninety dollars, Mr. Waterman. If you haven't done anything yet to earn it, you can just say so. I suppose your tone is just you being defensive, but I certainly don't appreciate your getting up on a high horse."

I wasn't about to tell Dunlap that Monnie Hinkle thought he was an FBI agent or at least informer and had advised me not to trust him.

"As a matter of fact, I was out of the office conducting an interview I hoped would provide some leads on Tom Heimer's fate or intentions or whereabouts. Unfortunately, my inquiries did not produce the desired results."

"Be that as it may," Dunlap said, "I do have some additional information that might be useful in locating Tom. That was the reason I had been trying without success to reach you."

"And now you have reached me. What did you find out?"

It occurred to me that Dunlap somehow knew that Monnie had his suspicions and had passed them on to me, and understood that that was why I was being so snippy.

"Someone told me that in the past, whenever Tom was in some kind of troublesome situation, he'd go see a homosexual man he went to high school with on this man's farm near Quakertown. I tried to reach this person, but he doesn't seem to have a listed telephone. Maybe you can track him down and see if possibly Tom is hiding out up there."

"What's the guy's name?"

"Bill Lathrop."

"I'll try to find a way to contact him or drive up there if I can't. Did you check with the Grange or the Bucks County ag agent?"

"I didn't think of that."

"I can do it."

"The farm is probably well known," Dunlap added. "It used to be a socialist commune."

"Socialist or just a bunch of Quakers?"

"No, real Norman Thomas or W.E.B. DuBois socialists. This was a number of years ago."

"How did you find out about this Lathrop guy?"

"Some friend of Tom's must have told me. Somebody who knew Tom when he was younger."

Or somebody who had seen his FBI file. Though if the FBI was really after Tom Heimer, why was I being used to track him down, if that was what was happening here? J. Edgar Hoover's resources were far vaster than mine.

I said, "I'll see what I can come up with, Mr. Dunlap. Meanwhile, I also have another duty to carry out today, a very sad one. Have you heard that a young man jumped off the Delaware River bridge last night?"

"No," he said with no hesitation, and I was sure he was lying. "What happened? Who was it?"

I told him it was Leslie Croyer, one of the gay men arrested at Stem t' Stern on Monday night, and that I had been trying to help him out of his legal difficulties.

"Oh, I am so sorry to hear that. My God, I hope Tom didn't do anything like that. That's one thing that didn't occur to me."

"No self-destructive urges?"

"Tom is not the type, no. Of course, you never know about people's inner demons, do you? I do know Tom has some extreme political ideas."

"He does?" *What could this have to do with suicide?*

"He has Marxist tendencies, actually. Or maybe I shouldn't really be mentioning that. I doubt if the city school board knows. Please don't mention to anyone that I said that. You yourself probably find it off-putting, and I hope it won't mean that you'll stop trying to locate Tom."

"You gave me ninety bucks, and I'm a capitalist."

"That's what I was hoping to hear."

I had to get going. I gave Dunlap my home number. I told him I'd check out the Quakertown farmer. I didn't tell Dunlap that I also planned on doing some checking up on him.

CHAPTER 17

Chester County didn't have a separate building for a morgue, just a couple of dungeon-like basement rooms in the Chester city hospital. The dizzying smell of formaldehyde, or whatever it was, made you want to look for a window to open or even crawl out of, except there wasn't one. The fluorescent lighting up among the pipes on the low ceiling—one of the six tubes was flickering and popping—made the living and the dead look the same, bled out and worthless.

Leslie Croyer's corpse had been tugged out of his refrigerated shelving on casters that needed oiling. A male attendant with a shaved head and a jagged scar across the side of his skull—a war injury?—pulled the shroud aside so that Byron Summerson could view the face of the young man he had ached for.

Though Croyer had been in the river for only a matter of hours, the refinery chemicals dumped in the Delaware, and maybe any hardy carp who'd happened by, had made a merciless mockery of the handsome young fellow's visage. Even I, however, recognized that this unlucky human being most likely had fairly recently been Leslie Croyer.

Summerson gave a single nod and then began to retch. The attendant quickly handed Summerson a basin that apparently was kept handy for this purpose.

I waited in an anteroom and paged through *The American Legion Magazine* while Summerson went into a lavatory and washed up. When he came out looking pale and frail, a matronly woman with a clipboard and no particular expression on her long face soon appeared, and he signed some documents.

Croyer's parents in Lock Haven had been notified by police up there and had made arrangements with a local funeral home. The body would be trucked upstate in a bag. Presumably a more dignified container awaited.

Summerson was quiet on the drive back up to the city. The sky had clouded over, but it was still close on ninety-two and almost too muggy for anybody with normal lungs to do much better than gasp for air. I had all the windows in the Plymouth rolled down. Conversation would have been difficult anyway, owing to the overheated air roaring in the front window of the car and out the back. I had added water to the radiator from Ted's spigot, reducing the odds that the car's engine would explode through the aged contraption's rusting hood.

If it had been Byron Summerson's intention to make me feel guilty over Croyer's suicide, he had to be brimming with satisfaction. In my head, I kept repeating to myself I had done what I could to deal with The Hat and the other courthouse crooks. I was a regular human being, not Captain Marvel, and if a connected guy and chum of the King of Denmark like Mike Stover couldn't budge the greedy and corrupt city bosses, how could I even make a dent?

But it nagged at me that I had failed. Summerson had led Croyer to believe I could get him out of this terrifying jam, and in Croyer's head the person who was his only hope had whiffed. I had explained to Summerson up front that Judge Stetson was probably too tough a nut to crack. But I had held out a smidgen of hope, and when that hope was dashed, Croyer couldn't take it and chose a violent death in the Delaware over having an announcement in the *Inquirer* or the *Evening Bulletin* that he was a sexual deviant. I had tried, but I couldn't get over that I was a part of this disgusting turn of events.

I didn't say anything to Summerson, but I was also mad at him for dragging me into this mess. Was he really so naïve to think that anybody less than some mob godfather, or the archbishop of Philly, or maybe General MacArthur could make a deal with the country club hoodlums who ran the city of Philadelphia? They were like Mussolini in the '30s, who was all-powerful before he got strung up.

And Leslie Croyer, I was pissed off at him as well. I felt sorry for the poor sap, in danger of not only losing his job but humiliating his family up in West Gum Stump, or whatever that place was. But why pile the whole steaming load on *my* shoulders?

The more I thought about it, the more I sped along fuming inside my hot brain. Though I didn't say anything to Summerson, sitting there staring straight ahead in the passenger seat beside me. At this point, what could he say or do? I'd keep the ninety dollars, pay my phone bill, and move along. Summerson was going back to Chestnut Hill, alone and forlorn, to whatever that strange small business of his was.

I offered to drive him out to his home, but he said no thanks, he'd take the bus from Center City. I wondered if he was concerned about being seen getting out of my prewar car in Chestnut Hill.

When I dropped Summerson off at a bus stop on the less tainted southern side of the Chinese wall, he said, "Thank you, Mr. Waterman, for your moral and utilitarian support. I do so very much appreciate it."

"Glad to help."

"When I have been informed as to funeral arrangements, I'll let you know."

I muttered, "You can save your breath," but he didn't hear me.

CHAPTER 18

The Bill Lathrop farm outside Quakertown wasn't hard to locate. The local ag office knew about it, and the middle-aged waitress at the diner where I had a grilled cheese and a milkshake said the place was famous. The farm had been a Jewish socialist commune forty years ago, and during both wars conscientious objectors sometimes stayed there before they were hauled off to jail.

Now the Lathrop place was just an ordinary corn and potatoes farm run by one guy from a local family. The waitress, whose name tag said she was Lorraine, told me that Bill Lathrop came into the diner sometimes.

"They say he's a communist," she told me, "but if you kid him about it, he's a good sport."

The two dozen or so acres of corn were already being picked, it looked like, and maybe the potatoes too. The farmhouse was the usual gray schist with some wooden outbuildings. There were sizable gaps in the wire fencing around the big barn, so apparently no livestock were being kept.

The man who came around the corner of the house as I approached it looked as if he'd been rolling around in the harvested crops. A slender, sun-singed blond guy of maybe fifty, his overalls had bits of dried corn debris all over them, and there were additional flecks in his whiskers and even his eyebrows. He was toting a bucket of something, and it didn't smell like Royal Pudding.

I introduced myself and said I'd been hired by Tom Heimer's apartment mate to locate Heimer, who seemed to have gone missing. The roommate, Trevor Dunlap, suggested I look up Lathrop, supposedly an old friend, to see if maybe Heimer was up here in Quakertown.

Lathrop listened without expression until I said Dunlap's name, and then he winced.

"I don't know where Tom is," Lathrop said evenly. "Sorry I can't help."

"Dunlap said in the past when Heimer has been in trouble, he sometimes turned to you for assistance. Did you know Tom was arrested in a gay bar raid Monday night?"

He stood still for a moment, still holding his bucket. "I heard something about it."

"From Tom?"

He set the bucket down. "I'm going to ask you something."

"Okay."

"Are you a federal agent?"

"No. If I was, I'd be required to show you ID."

"Not if you were working undercover."

It was occasions like this one where it would have made sense to flash my dishonorable discharge certificate, but it was back at the office. Instead I dug the photostat of my private investigator's license issued by the Pennsylvania Department of Labor and Industry out of my wallet and held up it for Lathrop to read. It had been through the discreet intercession of a closeted gay state senator in Harrisburg who I'd once helped out that I was able to hold a PI license despite what the Commonwealth of Pennsylvania viewed as my "moral turpitude," and the paper was real.

Lathrop said, "This looks fake."

"Tell Governor Duff."

"How come Dunlap hired a private investigator? Why didn't he go to the police?"

"He's gay and Heimer is gay, and the police aren't interested in homosexuals except to bloody our noses."

"Umm." Standing there in the bright sunshine, Lathrop and I were both perspiring, and I was a little sorry Bobby Carletti wasn't there to sample the tastes and aromas.

"Trevor Dunlap may be gay," Lathrop said after a moment, "but even if he is, he is not a gay man other gay men can trust."

"Heimer told you that?"

"Tom and others."

"What has Dunlap done to inspire mistrust?"

Lathrop seemed to think of something. "Let me make a phone call," he said. "Then maybe we can talk."

He left the bucket where it was, and I followed him around to a screened-in back porch. At his direction, I sat on a porch swing suspended by chains while he went into the house. I liked porch swings. Mom enjoyed sitting on the one on the front porch of the little house she and Dad had moved to up in Allentown to be near Aunt Thelma and Uncle Grant. Unsupervised kids could go wild on them, but grown-ups knew to be cautious and not rip the eye-hooks out of the overhead beams above, and since I was grown-up now, I swung sedately.

After three or four minutes, Lathrop emerged with a pitcher of water and two Mason jars to serve as glasses. He set them down on a small table next to the swing.

"Thanks for your patience. I've been reassured that you are not a fed."

"Like I said."

"You did. Can't be too careful."

"Who'd you call?"

"I called Tom. He'd heard of you."

"Aha."

Lathrop poured each of us a jar of cold water. An additive would have been nice, but I had no objections to simple hydration. I would have liked a smoke, but I didn't see an ashtray.

"Tom was here overnight," Lathrop said. "You missed him by a couple of hours. I can't tell you where he is, but he also heard from someone that you were working on the same thing he is working on and he wishes you well."

What was this? "What am I working on besides locating Tom? I did try to negotiate a lower payoff to Judge Stetson for another client. But to my everlasting regret, that didn't work out. Am I working on something else also?"

"Tom said he heard you were trying to find a way to neutralize The Hat and Ray Phipps. Aren't you?"

"The word does seem to be going around Philly that that's what I'm up to. But I'm not. The unavoidable truth is, nobody can. Those guys are entrenched. They are immovable. A Buddhist I met, a guy from India, says when it comes to things in life like Judge Stetson and Ray Phipps, you just have to figure they'll get their comeuppance in their next life. And if you and I are lucky, and we've built up enough karmic merit, we'll be around to watch."

Lathrop gave me a funny look. "Do you believe that human beings are really that powerless?"

"In a lot of cases, you bet I do."

"Tom doesn't believe that, and neither do I."

"Well, I wish you fellows all the luck in the world with this particular set of unusually ugly circumstances. Me, I'm about worn out by it all."

I didn't bring up that I had tried to work out a deal for Leslie Croyer and, having failed, had helped make Croyer give up not just on me but on everybody else in the entire world.

"We *know* we are not powerless on this particular occasion," Lathrop said calmly. "Tom is confident he really can neutralize both Phipps and The Hat. And why is that? It's because he *has* something on Judge Stetson. Not occupational, but something of a personal nature. Once he nails a few matters down, he's sure he'll be able to extort the extortionists."

"And people think I'm in on *that*?"

He shrugged. "It sure looks that way."

Sweet Jesus, I thought. Bobby Carletti telling me I was up to here in deep shit was no longer sounding anywhere near far-fetched.

CHAPTER 19

Lathrop told me Tom Heimer wasn't ready to make his move just yet. But when he was ready, he'd get in touch with me and maybe I'd want to be in on it. I said yeah, or maybe I'd just want to watch from a safe distance, a safe distance in the case of Ray Phipps and The Hat probably being North Africa.

I asked Lathrop why Heimer hadn't informed his school that he needed to take some time off, maybe say he was ill. Lathrop said Tom had told him he thought the school's phone was being tapped by the FBI and his calls could be traced. I knew left-wingers could be paranoid, but I was starting to think maybe they had their reasons.

I drove back into Philly and parked behind Ted's. Up in my steam room of an office, I had a small nip. It was late Friday afternoon and the Pennsy commuter trains outside my window were starting to haul the city's buttoned-up corporation grinds away from the human riffraff and blistering pavements of the city out to their leafy retreats in Ardmore and Berwyn and Malvern for the weekend. I wondered if the cops had any new torment-the-fags operation dreamed up for Friday or Saturday night. I supposed there would be apprehension around town that that might happen, and a lot of gay guys would stay home or do private get-togethers.

I tried phoning Trevor Dunlap at the mint and reached him in the security department. He hadn't left yet for the weekend, or maybe the people guarding all those fresh new Hamiltons and Franklins were required to keep an eye out seven days a week.

"I hope it's okay my calling you at work," I said.

"Yes. This is important. Any luck locating Tom?"

"I'm afraid not. I met his friend in Quakertown, but Tom wasn't there."

"That's too bad. Damn. And I don't really have any other leads I can suggest."

"I guess I could check with Tom's teachers' union local to see if they're aware of any missing funds. But I don't want to cast suspicion where none is warranted."

"No, I wouldn't do that," Dunlap said. "Not yet at any rate. I'd give that one a day or two."

"Yeah, and then maybe even notify the police if Tom doesn't turn up anywhere."

"Well, I don't know about that. You know how the Philadelphia cops are about homosexuals. Though, of course, if worse comes to worst ... "

"Let's play it by ear, then. I'll see what other leads I can develop. And you let me know, Mr. Dunlap, if you pick up on anything. Maybe Heimer will surprise you and just show up at your apartment and have some simple explanation as to his recent whereabouts."

"That's what I'll hope for," Dunlap said, and he hung up, leaving me thinking, *What is this fed up to?*

I didn't know anybody in the FBI. A couple of officers I had known when I was in the police had become agents, but these were not men I was chummy with at the time. I did know a lawyer, though, a straight guy named Dale Rowles, who practiced in federal district court. He had represented a number of bank robbers, the type of criminals the FBI was interested in when they weren't chasing communists, and I thought maybe he knew about the inner workings of the local office of the bureau.

Rowles was also well known among people in Philly who followed jazz, because he was a second cousin or something to Jimmy Rowles, Benny Goodman's current piano player, and Dale traveled long distances to hear any Goodman band or small group play.

I was lucky when I called Rowles's office. He was about to head out for the weekend and picked up the phone himself. We talked for a few minutes about how the bands were struggling in the postwar economy. He said a new thing, long-playing records, was soon to be introduced, and maybe it would help the bands hang on. I said I'd heard something about that. Anyway, we agreed, the small combos were doing okay.

Getting to the point, I told Rowles I was working on a missing person case, and my client was a US Mint employee who I thought might be FBI, but if he was, he wasn't telling me so.

I said, "Ever hear of a Trevor Dunlap?"

"Yeah, if it's the guy I'm thinking of. A Treasury agent assigned to the mint. Sure—how many Trevor Dunlaps can there be on the federal payroll?"

"You've run into him professionally?"

"He was a prosecution witness against a client of mine, Lazlo Strunk, who the government claimed held up the First National Bank of Pottsville. Dunlap ID'd some marked bills that were in Mr. Strunk's possession, as I recall."

"Did he do it?"

"Dunlap?"

"No, Lazlo Strunk. Rob the bank."

"Not to my knowledge."

"Anyway, none of that makes Dunlap FBI."

"No, but I had a similar case more recently where I expected

Dunlap to turn up again as a government witness, and he didn't. I asked the prosecutor. He said Dunlap had moved on, and he was working on a special project. I can ask around if you want me to."

"If you could do it discreetly, that would help out. Come up with a pretext."

There was a pause and I guessed Rowles was either making a note in that way lawyers do, or lighting a cigarette. He said, "I'll get back to you."

"One other thing, Dale. I know you work the federal courts, but you probably hear things about the state courts. Do you know about a judge named Harold Stetson?"

Rowles exhaled heartily. It had been a cigarette. He said, "Oh my, yes. The Hat."

"That's the man."

"He's a criminal."

"That's what all of gay Philadelphia is all too painfully aware of. Why is this guy still on the bench?"

"You tell me."

"And his bag man is this Ray Phipps, the court clerk. Do you know about him?"

"I've heard talk."

"Somebody who was the victim of a gay bar raid this week claims he has something on Judge Stetson that will bring his criminal career on the bench to an end," I said. "It's something apparently of a personal nature. Any idea what that could possibly be?"

Another pause to reflect. "Nothing I know of offhand. But I could ask around. My wife is friends with a woman who knows somebody who once had an affair with Ray Phipps. She might have an idea of whatever bad thing it could be with the judge."

"Please ask."

"People complain about Philly being such a hick town, and they run off to big, bad, exciting New York. But living in a place where everybody knows everybody else's business can be useful on occasion."

I said, "Three cheers."

CHAPTER 20

After a tuna salad supper at Horn and Hardart's, I walked around in the heat. Cairo was even worse in the summer, but that's because it was in the Sahara Desert. What was Philadelphia's excuse?

I couldn't see any moon or stars in the sky over Rittenhouse Square, and it felt a little like rain. But the only water falling from above was dripping from somebody's leaky window air conditioner in an apartment building on the east side of the square. A lot of the people in the building who didn't have air conditioners had their windows open, and music was coming from somewhere on the second or third floor, Perry Como wending his way through "Chi-baba, Chi-baba." The song's words seemed to be made up, but not made-up words that were fun like Ella Fitzgerald's. Perry sounded as if he was talking to himself while pushing a grocery cart around the A&P.

There were a couple of cops strolling around the outer perimeter of the square with their billy clubs dangling from their belts, but they weren't hitting anybody over the head with them at the moment. Several of the benches were occupied by solitary men with that antennas-out look while on other benches couples or small groups chitchatted.

I saw a couple of guys I knew, and we chewed over the

recent raids, and how all of gay Philly was perplexed as to what was going on. Nobody could figure it out.

A young man named Elmer who I knew slightly said to me, "One of the girls arrested in the Stem raid committed suicide; did you hear that?"

I said I had.

"She couldn't afford to pay off The Hat, and she was afraid her family in Gettysburg was going to read in the *Inquirer* she was a homo. She jumped off the Camden bridge and when they found her, her head was missing. They think it was chewed off by catfish. This is what you have to put up with to be queer in the City of Brotherly Love. Me, I'd move to New York, but is it really any better up there? Maybe in Greenwich Village, I suppose."

I overheard some other people talking about the bar raids, and one said, "I bet Polly-Wolly's stays closed for a long time. The owner is in the hospital in an oxygen tent."

I walked over to Sal's and stopped in for some Jim Beam in a glass that had never contained sandwich spread.

Serving me, Sal said, "It's a little slow tonight. The girls are antsy."

"With reason."

"Everybody's afraid to pick up the *Inquirer* in the morning, or the *Bulletin*, on account of they might be in there, called a pervert for Aunt Margaret to read about."

"Aunt Margaret or the principal of the school where they teach."

"Wouldn't want the kiddies being taught by a faggot."

"Heaven forbid."

"Even though if they fired all the homo teachers, they'd have to shut the schools down."

I said, "I had a teacher in ninth grade who acted like a big sis. But he had a wife and about half a dozen kids."

"In eleventh grade I had one who I think really was one.

Young, really built. He liked to lean over the boys and check their homework. I'd get a hard-on every time, and I think he noticed. But he never did anything. The guy knew better."

I told Sal I was looking for one of the bar raid victims who was now missing, and I asked him if he knew Tom Heimer.

"Yeah, he's an industrial arts teacher. Good guy. A little on the serious side, though."

"I'm trying to track him down. What about Heimer's roommate, name of Trevor Dunlap?"

"Boyfriend?"

"No, just sharing an apartment."

"Is he missing too?"

"No, he's the one who hired me. He works at the mint. In security."

"Oh. Older guy? Skinny? Gray head of hair? Well dressed? Not that it helps in this bimbo's case."

"I think so."

"If it's the guy, he's a bad egg," Sal said, picking up a bar rag and swiping the already clean counter. "Picked up one of our regulars one time in here. Then didn't want to have sex or anything at all. He just asked a lot of questions about, did this guy, Sam, know who was gay who worked at the mint? Sam got suspicious and made an excuse. I haven't seen your guy since then. This was maybe a year or so ago."

"Is Sam in here now?" I asked.

"No, haven't seen him since the raids."

A guy who'd just come in Sal's front door walked directly over to us. He was burly with gray whiskers and had the dress and look of a longshoreman. I had a feeling I'd tricked with him at least once before, maybe before the war. Anyway, he recognized me.

"Clifford Waterman, hey! Jesus Christ, I was just talking to somebody who's looking for you. Amos Leary?"

"Yeah, I know Amos."

"I guess I can tell you, you're gonna find out soon enough."

"Find out what?"

"The building where your office is, on Cuthbert."

"Yeah?"

"It's on fire."

CHAPTER 21

Somebody had shoved the Plymouth clear of the building before the back wall came down, so my insurance wasn't going to get me a new car. I was actually able to drive it away just after dawn with not much damage to the old heap besides some dents in the roof and hood and a few blisters on the prewar superior paint job. When my car saw me coming, the thing practically leaped into my arms.

The crazy thing is, the thing that most burned me up—if I may use that expression—was the loss of my army dishonorable discharge certificate. That piece of paper said more about who I actually was than all the other documents about me put together. It practically ruined my life, but it was also a piece of paper that announced to me the honest-to-God's truth about myself. It had taken the United States Government to make me totally face up to, and really get to know, the person I was. It had not been the army's intention—that's for goddamn sure—but my dishonorable discharge had actually made an honest man of me. After Uncle Sam had his way, I was no longer a sneak. And I knew the army well enough to know that getting a replacement certificate to that effect was going to be a job and a half. Would my congressman help? It was going to be fun to see.

By 3 a.m. the fire was under control, and by five it was all but extinguished. The front of the four-story business block was the least damaged, structurally unsound but with the façade intact. The rear, where my office had been, and where the fire had started, was a heap of smoking debris. I climbed up on the Chinese wall at one point, had a long look, and thought, *Well, what the fuck, that's that.*

My first thought as to the cause was that it was a grease fire at Ted's that had gotten out of hand. Or maybe I had somehow dropped a lighted Lucky in my wastebasket. Or—this one got its jaws around my overheated brainpan and refused to let go— the building was torched by somebody who wanted to warn me away from whatever was going on in gay Philly or even put me all the way out of business. So it was no big surprise when a queer fireman I knew, Steven Kresge, took me aside after things had begun to quiet down. He told me not to say the information came from him, but the fire marshal had already figured out that the fire had been purposely set in the rear stairwell with the aid of an accelerant.

I managed to make room in my wild and woolly emotions for some sympathy for Ted Panagopoulos and his wife, Stella, whose luncheonette, in the family for thirty years, was kaput. They stood staring silently at the wreckage of their daily lives until around three in the morning when one of their daughters led them away.

The neighborhood was quieter than I'd ever known it to be, partly on account of the late hour but also because the Pennsy had had to suspend trains from coming or going at Broad Street Station. Everybody taking a train to or from Philly had to do it at Thirtieth Street. For several hours firemen had been up on the Chinese wall shooting water at the flames. They didn't begin rolling up their hoses along the railroad tracks until almost dawn. A big crowd had gathered earlier, but most of them were gone by sunrise.

I recognized a number of people among the gawkers, some

of them patrons at Stem t' Stern, a few blocks up the street. I pretended not to notice them and moved nonchalantly away. I was worried somebody would ask me if I had any ideas as to how the fire had started and if it had been set on purpose, and if so who did it and why? I was afraid that if I talked about this subject, I might start shaking and wouldn't be able to stop.

At one point, after the crowd had thinned, a fireman sent in my direction a reporter for the *Inquirer*, a middle-aged guy with a big red schnoz and a press card in his hatband, who had been asking around for people who'd been tenants in the destroyed building.

"Clifford Waterman, private investigator," I told the reporter in answer to his first question.

"Your office was on the fourth floor?"

"In the back, by the railroad."

"But you were not in your office when the fire broke out?"

"I wouldn't normally be in there on a Friday night, nuh uh."

"So are the contents of your office a total loss?"

"That appears to be the case."

"So your—what?—files and records for your business are all gone?"

"Yeah. It's gonna be a pain."

"Anything else of value?"

"My army discharge document. I'm not sure I even know how to go about replacing it."

The reporter noticed his photographer standing not far away and called him over.

"Eddie, this guy's a vet. Where'd you serve, Clifford?"

"North Africa."

"Whoa. Rommel?"

"Idriss."

He asked me how to spell that and I told him. The guy with the camera was angling to get me in a frame with a fire truck in the background and then took a couple of flashes.

"How come you're still out here, Clifford? You don't expect to salvage anything, do you?"

"My car's out back. They say it's okay, and I'm waiting for them to let me go collect it."

"That was lucky. I'm hearing rumors that the fire was set. Have you heard that?"

"No kidding?"

"Yeah, I'm trying to get a confirmation, but the state fire marshal could yada-yada for days. I'm going to have to go with what I have. Hey, as a PI you must have pissed off a few people over the years, Clifford. Think there's anybody mad enough at you these days to burn down the building that has your office in it?"

I said I did a lot of divorce work, so, yeah, I supposed that was possible. The reporter and his photographer friend both nodded knowingly—sometimes divorces could be a bitch—and then they thanked me and wandered away.

CHAPTER 22

I tried to sleep, but the phone kept practically jangling off the cradle. I could have taken my winter coat out of mothballs and wrapped it around the instrument, or I could have ripped the phone out of the wall, thrown it out the window, and then jumped out after it. But I thought Tom Heimer might call about his plan to do in Ray Phipps and The Hat—I'd left my number for him with Tom Lathrop—so I dragged myself out of bed and answered every call. Most were friends showing sympathy. Word had gotten around that the building with my office in it had gone up in flames. Rumors had spread far and wide that it might have been the doings of a firebug, and whenever anybody mentioned this, I said, yeah, I heard that, too.

Amos Leary was one of the people who called, during his ten-minute cigarette break at the Wanamaker's shoe department, and then Monnie Hinkle. He'd just gotten in after playing a band gig and then going out with the musicians. Amos and Monnie both asked if I thought the fire had anything to do with me, and I said, well, it was always a possibility.

Walking back home from the fire—I'd stashed the Plymouth in a space behind Sal's he sometimes let me use—I scrounged up the eighteen cents for a fresh pack of Luckies and then went through a third of the pack while palavering on the phone. I knew some people called cigarettes cancer sticks, but what was cancer next to being a nervous wreck? I got out some corn flakes, but Monnie and I had used all the milk the day before. So I made do with another corn product, an amber fluid I poured into a clean Kraft sandwich-spread jar, and this helped me settle down and think straight, or so it felt at the time, and I do believe in placebos.

Tom Heimer didn't call, but Trevor Dunlap did. He complained he'd tried to call my office, but the phone was out of order.

I said, "That's because the building my office was in burned down last night."

"Oh, my God! Are you serious? I hadn't heard that."

Why was I a hundred percent sure he was lying? "There are rumors it was arson, but I don't think there's anything official yet."

"Well. Boy oh boy. So I guess you haven't even had time to think about where Tom Heimer has disappeared to."

"Nuh uh."

"Which is understandable."

Weirdly, I wanted to place the phone's earpiece under my nose to find out if I could smell kerosene on the hand Dunlap was holding his receiver with. This is how tired I was. Instead, I told him I had a couple of other ideas I was going to pursue as soon as I had had a few hours' sleep. This was a crock, but it got him off the phone. Then I actually did conk out for about half an hour before the phone blew up in my ear again. This time it was Byron Summerson.

"Mr. Waterman, I am so, so sorry about your office. What a devastating thing to have to go through on top of everything else. I just wanted you to know you have my deepest sympathy."

"Thank you, Byron. Luckily, there was no loss of life or limb. So there's that."

"Will you open another office? That could work out well for

you, inasmuch as the old location was far from ideal."

"I guess I'll have to. Maybe I'll wait and see if Ted Panagopoulos reopens his luncheonette and try to get a place above him again."

Why was I razzing this guy? He'd just lost the young man he had a giant crush on to suicide. And here I was, one of the causes of the guy killing himself, reminding Summerson he was too prissy to cope with the smell of a couple of wienies in hot sauce.

"I know I've asked a lot of you," Summerson said, "and if I may, I am going to ask you for an additional kindness. I'll be happy to pay all your expenses, plus of course another ninety dollars."

Now what? But the ninety did snag my interest. "Tell me what you have in mind."

"Leslie's funeral will be Monday morning in Lock Haven. I was wondering if you might be willing to accompany me to it. A member of Leslie's theater company will be coming along, and we could all three take the train up tomorrow afternoon and stay at a local hostelry I've been told about, and then return to Philly Monday after the funeral. Might you fit that into your schedule? I do realize that your life has been seriously upended by the loss of your normal place of business."

I was immediately suspicious. "Why me, Byron? I mean, didn't Leslie have work friends? And, as you said, friends among his theater people?"

He grew quiet. "The thing of it is," he finally said, "it would have been important to Leslie that his friends and associates from Philadelphia were people who—when they go up to Lock Haven and meet his family and friends—can pass."

"For white? You are white." But I knew what he meant.

"For straight. A lot of Leslie's theater friends are a little bit—well, you know."

Only two things kept me from hanging up on Summerson.

One was, all of a sudden it seemed like a good idea to disappear from Philly for a few days. Clear my own thinking and let The Hat/Ray Phipps-situation dust settle. Also, even though thinking about it made me mad all over again, I still felt guilty about letting Croyer down to the point where the poor sap actually ended up taking his own life. He owed *me* something for dragging me into this ridiculous bullshit with Judge Stetson in the first place. But I owed *him* something for so rashly telling him to find a way to cough up the five hundred and just get out of my life.

I said, "Yeah, I guess I could do it. Would I have to wear splints on my wrists?"

"No, from what Leslie told me, you'll fit right in in Lock Haven just as you are, Mr. Waterman. Well, thank you so, so much. I am so relieved. I was dreading the whole experience, and now I am less apprehensive."

He gave me info about meeting at Broad Street Station Sunday morning at 11:40. He said a woman named Abigail Pabst, a local actress, would be coming along with us. The word *actress* should have been a tip-off as to what was to come, but at the time it sailed right over my head.

CHAPTER 23

I found out that the room at the Spruce Street boardinghouse had just been vacated and it was available for me to get some rest. I slogged over there—the phone was ringing at my place as I closed the door—and aimed a floor fan somebody had brought in at the bed. The oscillating fan on the dresser was backing and forthing, too, still scanning the room for kamikaze Japs. The bed sheets had taken quite a beating during the night—I wondered who the happy couple, or thruple, or quadruple, were—and I tugged them off, tossed them into a hamper, and put down clean ones from the dresser.

I showered in the shared bathroom and came back to the room and hit the bed. I have no memory of the next five hours. I know I dreamed of Cairo and going over to look at the Sphinx and wondering what he was thinking about and what he was planning on doing next, if anything. I also dreamed of visiting the pyramids at Giza and being led around on a camel with TWA saddlebags and falling off and breaking my neck and being paralyzed from the chin down. Some of those things had actually happened during the war, minus the injury.

I woke up at ten after three in the afternoon with a headache. A hit of my stash—hair of the dog—helped with the pain.

I got up to make a call. There was no phone in the room,

merely a pay phone down in the entryway. Quakertown was not a local call, but it still only cost me a quarter.

"The building my office was in was torched last night," I told Bill Lathrop, "so I've been out of commission. I don't know if Tom Heimer has tried to reach me or not."

"I heard about the fire on Cuthbert, but I didn't know that was your building. Holy bejesus! You weren't in it, were you?"

"Nobody was. The luncheonette down on the street had just closed up. So, has Tom been in touch since I saw you yesterday?"

"I had a quick call last night from him saying he was on his way somewhere and I might not hear from him for a day or two. But I've been away from the phone a lot, so he might have called. You caught me coming in to rehydrate. This heat is bad for the corn, and it's even worse for the man who grows the corn."

"Tom was traveling out of the area?"

"Maybe not real far away, but that was my impression."

I guessed that Heimer's travels meant something, though I had no idea what, so I asked Lathrop. "And it's something to do with The Hat and Ray Phipps—dirt Tom is digging up or whatever?"

"That's what he told me. He sounded pretty sure he was onto something that was really going to make a difference for homosexuals in the city of Philadelphia. I'm as curious as you are, Clifford."

I doubted that was true. "I'm guessing that Judge Stetson and Phipps are Philly old boys and not from someplace else. So I wonder where Heimer is off to."

It was then I decided it was time, or past time, for me to do some checking on my own on the backgrounds of the two archvillains of gay Philly.

"I'll let you know if I hear anything," Lathrop said. "Anyway, I know Tom plans on contacting you. He thinks you might have some of the skills that will be needed to bring his plans to fruition."

"Which ones?"

"Which plans?"

"No, which skills? I can suck dick and I can parallel park."

He laughed. "I think you're being modest."

"Modest? I was bragging."

The operator was about to ask for another quarter, but before I rang off I told Lathrop I'd be upstate for a few days and I'd check back with him to find out if Heimer was attempting to reach me.

I dragged myself back over to Locust and was relieved to see that the building I called home was not a smoldering heap of ashes. As I opened the door to my apartment, the phone was (still?) ringing, but I ignored it.

When the caller gave up, I placed calls to a few people to see if any more official harass-the-homos events had gone on overnight. Not surprisingly, some had. No bar raids, but a lot more than usual of the normal name-calling and shoving people around and even arresting them in parks and other outdoor cruising locales. Two people in a parked car in Fairmount Park had been charged with "morals offenses." This meant anything people were doing sexually that didn't personally appeal to the arresting officers.

Except for the Fairmount Park report, all the bad anti-homo stuff seemed to be in Center City, especially north of South Street and up and around the railroad wall. Did that mean anything? It was an area where I both lived and worked, but despite the fact my office had been purposely incinerated the night before, I decided that whatever was going on was much bigger than me. Or was it? I was more confused than ever, another milestone in the career of Clifford Waterman, private investigator.

CHAPTER 24

Charleen Backus was an editor at *The Saturday Evening Post* and lived over on Camac Street in an eighteenth-century house about the size of a bread box. Her girlfriend, Dorothy, a pilot who had ferried planes from aircraft factories to air force bases during the war, had died in a Pennsylvania Turnpike car crash just after V-J Day, fate being stupid and cruel. I knew Charleen's dad had been a state rep from North Philly for a long time and that she knew the ins and outs and who was who in political Philadelphia and Harrisburg, the state's dismal capital city. I called and asked her if I could stop by for an hour, late afternoon, and she said sure.

Camac was one of those streets that hadn't changed in two hundred years except for the addition of electric lights and a lack of parking spaces. I hiked over at five, and Charleen greeted me with the offer of some kind of strange drink she made with ice smashed in a towel with a hammer, lime juice, the herb basil, and ginger. All I knew of ginger was ale and sometimes a girl's name. It was not the refreshment I hoped to be offered, but when I tried it I could see getting used to it.

We sat in her dim little living room, which had a window air conditioner running that cooled the room but sounded like a troop carrier trying to get up a long hill. It was lucky neither of us was hard of hearing.

Charleen was sixty or so, on the chunky side but with no apparent qualms about it, considering the way she flung herself around the place. She had big gray eyes that sized you up and a wild head of black and gray hair. Aunt Thelma would have asked Charleen if she had never heard of a perm.

Charleen knew about last night's fire and that I was one of the displaced tenants. "The word is it was arson, so I hope it has nothing to do with you, Cliff. Could it?"

It was a question I was going to have to get used to.

"It might've. I'm working on something. That's why I need to talk to you. I mean, to somebody who knows the political cast of characters around the city."

"Oh, well. A Philly pol with a gas can and a match? Let's start making a list."

"The connection might be indirect. Or there might not be any connection at all. What do you know about Judge Harold Stetson?"

Charleen said something like *foof* and rummaged around for a cigarette. I lit one, too.

She said, "The guy they call 'The Hat.'"

"That's the one."

"It's the name, plus I guess he wears one."

"It's well known he's totally corrupt, and yet he's still on the bench. He comes down especially hard on gay men. He's not just moralistic like in Sunday school; he's really mean and sadistic. Currently, Stetson and his bag man, a court clerk by the name of Ray Phipps, are making guys pay five hundred dollars to get disorderly conduct charges dropped after bar raids. It's a total racket. What do you know about this guy, and how come he seems to be untouchable?"

Charleen gulped down some of her drink that, for me, was starting to taste the way shoe polish smells.

"I've been hearing about his scam for years," she said. "How

Stetson hangs on, I don't know. Originally he was appointed by Governor James in thirty-eight or -nine when the judge on Stetson's bench back then unexpectedly croaked while enjoying a cocktail during his longer-than-appropriate lunch hour. But the Republican machine liked Stetson, and most of the voters do, too. So, he keeps getting elected. Of course it would help if the Dems put up a candidate besides somebody's brother-in-law whose idea of campaigning is to pass out cases of Johnny Walker at Christmas and country club memberships on Easter to party ward committeemen. The voters sometimes show at least a modicum of sense."

"So Stetson is a Philly boy, not an immigrant from Wilkes-Barre or somewhere?"

"West Philly or possibly Upper Darby. His family was in the coal business. He was in private practice for twenty years or so defending a variety of miscreants, generally those well-fixed enough for Stetson to maintain a house with tennis courts and a pool in Wynnewood. His best known case was in thirty-five or -six. Laurence Pickelner, the head of Pickelner Ball Bearings, was arrested for an incident involving a couple of boys of tender age. Stetson got him off, arguing that his company was too important to the city's employment picture with the Depression still going on to have him locked up for years while the company unraveled. Some people were outraged at the time, but Pickelner had a lot of important friends, and they turned out to be quite helpful to Stetson later on. Who knows? Maybe they still are."

"Underaged boys, huh? Could that also possibly be an interest of the judge himself?"

"I never heard that. No, Harold is a lady's man. We're around the same age, and when I was in my twenties I was aware of him, and I knew that in that particular area of human endeavor he cut quite a swath. He eventually married a debutante from Elkins Park, Mae Quayle, and as far as I know they're still together."

"Any hanky-panky on the side?"

"That I wouldn't know. Though in the suburbs, you have to figure. Here in the city we're supposed to be the decadent ones, but girls I know at work at *The Post* assure me that among straight people it's Bala-Cynwyd that's Sodom and Gomorrah."

"Being in my line of work, this is not news to me."

"Love in the sand trap on the seventeenth hole."

I took another sip of the crushed-ice Shinola. "What about Ray Phipps, the court clerk and bag man? Know anything about him?"

"Only that he also has a posh house in Wynnewood that people wonder how he paid for on a court clerk's salary. He drives a big white Packard, and his wife has a Caddy you could fit all the Phillies in comfortably and maybe the A's, too. I know about Phipps because I have a legal secretary chum whose boss has to appear in that courtroom once in a while, and they talk about how rotten that whole situation is. Nobody understands why someone hasn't put a stop to it."

"Maybe it's the ball bearing king. Is Phipps also from Philly originally?"

"Out west, I think. Altoona?"

"What's his background out there? Any idea?"

"No, he's been in Philly for fifteen or twenty years."

"Don't mention this," I said, "for my sake, or even for your own well-being. But I know of a guy who claims to have some kind of incriminating personal information on Stetson. The guy hasn't let me in on it yet what the thing is. Any idea, Charleen, what type of guilty secret that could possibly involve the judge?"

She laughed. "I want to say that it's he's both a blackmailer and an extortionist. But of course that's no secret."

"Yeah. It must be something even worse. Or at least something that somebody with power and authority *thinks* is worse."

"I guess you'd have to figure out who has any control over that court and then know what their values are. Their values or their fears."

So that was something to think about while I ambled back over to Locust Street under the lowering sun, stopping along the way for a roll of breath mints.

CHAPTER 25

Sunday morning I picked up an *Inquirer* on the way to Broad Street Station and had a quick look-see. The Cuthbert Street fire had made the front page below the fold. The only photos were of the forlorn Panagopouloses standing in the light of the blaze and of flames shooting out of the roof. I did get my name mentioned as a displaced business tenant. It said I was a war veteran who had seen action in North Africa in the Idriss campaign.

Byron Summerson was already at the station when I arrived and had bought three tickets to Lock Haven and back. He introduced me to Abigail Pabst, who'd be coming along. A comely young redheaded woman of twenty-five or so, she was done up in a handsome blue skirt with pleats and a pretty white blouse.

She said, "Are you going as yourself, Clifford?"

I said, "Up to a point," and she chuckled.

"I'm going to have a hard time at first responding when anybody addresses me as Beverly. But I'll just pretend I'm in a play and that's my character. I'll rely primarily on my stage experience."

We were heading toward the platform where our train, the Buffalo Flyer, was scheduled to leave in about fifteen minutes. Summerson kept glancing at me and looking a little nervous, and I soon knew why.

"So," I said, "you're showing up at the funeral as somebody named Beverly?"

"Beverly Andrews. Leslie's fiancé."

I glanced over at Summerson, who looked straight ahead and twitched.

I said, "Oh, so Leslie's friends and family are under the impression he was engaged to be married?"

"I'm supposed to be extremely distraught. Which won't be all that hard. I really liked Leslie, and I'm just sick about what happened. We once did a scene together from *Kiss and Tell*, and he was so adorable. I really am going to miss the guy. He was always so nice. So many of us in the theater group wish we could have talked to him before he did what he did. It was all just so horribly unnecessary."

"Had a date been set for the wedding?"

"I'm supposed to say we were going to announce the date in April."

"Ah. Can I ask, who wrote your lines for you, Abigail? I mean Beverly."

"I did," Summerson now piped up. "I did so based on things Leslie had told me about his family and what would be expected of him. I suppose you are irked, Mr. Waterman, and in some sense I can appreciate how you would be. Leslie was a homosexual, like you and me, and of course he was unlikely to marry, not that such a course of action would be in any way unprecedented. It frequently happens. But really, at this point, what difference can any of that possibly make? Let's allow the Croyer family to mourn the loss of this wonderful young man in as trouble-free a manner as possible. Does that not make sense to you?"

I briefly shut my eyes and thought of the ninety dollars.

In the coach, Summerson took a window seat, and Abigail— "Beverly"—sat on the aisle on account of, she said, she would need to get up occasionally to "visit the ladies'." I sat on the seat across the aisle from her—a necessity for me too. I would need to traipse up to the smoker from time to time, preparing my frame of mind for my twenty-four hours in Lock Haven.

In Harrisburg an elderly Negro with a basket came through the car selling ham sandwiches and I asked for a couple. Summerson and Pabst had one each, and, as promised, he paid.

The Flyer didn't exactly fly, but it clanked and rumbled steadily northward along the wide Susquehanna and then the river's West Branch, stopping in small towns and then a bigger one, Williamsport, which looked sizably populated from the train window. The coach's air-conditioning, if it had any, was on the fritz, but we slid the windows partway down. When a passenger seated near us got hit in the eye with some flying soot and complained, I started getting sentimental over my office by the tracks that was lost forever.

We passed the Piper Aircraft factory just after four—you could see a lot of little yellow Piper Cubs in a field—and then slowed down and screeched to a halt by the Lock Haven station, a one-story, mud-colored brick job that crouched near the side of the tracks. Across the tracks from the station were a couple of dingy three-floor hotels with neon beer signs hanging off them: Peck's and the St. Cloud. They were a far cry from the Belleview-Stratford, or even the Spruce Street rooming house, and I hoped for dear life we would not be staying in one of them.

Leslie Croyer's parents, Charles and Flo, were there to greet us. There were brief howdy-dos with Summerson and me, but it was "Beverly" that the couple embraced as they both wept. The two middle-aged parents, he on the stout side, she skinny, clung to the actress for two or three minutes, shaking, with tears running down their faces. The train was about to pull out for the rest of its trip to the northwest, and I thought about jumping on it and riding on up to Buffalo, a city I had never visited. I could go over and catch a glimpse of Niagara Falls.

"We are so happy to be able to look at your face," Flo Croyer said, when she was finally able to speak. "We have been praying for this moment for weeks. Not weeks, months!"

"This is not the way we pictured it happening," Charles Croyer said. "But, at least, Beverly, here you are!"

I could feel myself getting red in the face. What I really wanted to do was wring Leslie Croyer's neck. But it was too late for that. If he hadn't jumped, after seeing this craziness I might have shoved him.

Summerson, Beverly, and I each placed our small valises in the trunk of the Croyers' Chevy and then squeezed into the back seat. As they drove us to our hotel—on the river, they said—Flo asked us a lot of questions about working for the insurance company, where we were all employed, and did we know so-and-so and so-and-so, who had thoughtfully had flowers delivered? Summerson looked mortified and hemmed and hawed. Beverly was a natural, though, and made things up off the cuff.

We soon got to the hotel, the Fallon House, on Water Street. The place looked respectable, a lot of white brick with a long front porch furnished with rockers and dozens of potted red geraniums in boxes hanging from the railings. Signs showed that the Kiwanis Club and Rotary met there weekly in the dining room, so I figured we were unlikely to get poisoned.

The Croyers parked and walked in with us while we checked in. Flo knew the front desk clerk, an older man named Jerry, and told him we were here for Leslie's funeral. She said two of us were Leslie's good friends and Beverly was actually Leslie's fiancée. Then Flo began to cry again. Charles comforted his wife and told Jerry he was sure the Fallon would take good care of us.

Jerry expressed his condolences to Summerson, Beverly, and me. Then he said, "It's so sad. There's so much of it going around now. And you never know who it could strike next. And it's the young who are the most susceptible."

The three of us were at a loss for words, but Flo helped us out. She said, "Yes, polio must be about the cruelest disease ever to afflict the human race. Leslie was the third Lock Haven boy to fall victim, and it just breaks your heart to think of who might succumb next."

CHAPTER 26

The buffet supper at the Croyer homestead on Fairview Street was confusing. Not the food—a lot of dishes friends and family had brought in were my favorites, like noodles baked in Campbell's cream of mushroom soup—but the conversation made me feel a little punch-drunk. Some of the mourners seemed to think that Leslie Croyer had died in an accidental drowning, others were under the impression he had polio, and some said, oh, it was both. Nobody mentioned jumping off a bridge.

Although a good number of Croyer relatives attended the sad event, there were no brothers or sisters of the dead youth. Leslie Croyer had been an only child.

Of us Philadelphia folks, Beverly should have been having the roughest time at the supper. Though whenever I saw her yackety-yacking with the female cousins and family friends, she seemed to be holding her own. I caught her eye once, but she didn't let on anything.

Summerson and I chewed the fat with the men, the main topics being the Phils and the A's. Most of us agreed that it might be time for Connie Mack to retire. He had been managing the A's since 1901 and it was starting to show. Somebody said, "Change the name of Shibe Park to Connie Mack Stadium and send the old coot on his way."

The Reverend Lyle Pilsner, pastor of the Evangelical United Brethren Church, paid a call while the desserts were being put out, and everybody hushed up while he recited a prayer. A balding middle-aged gent with the paunch of a bank's president and the gaze of its loan officer, the minister prayed for Leslie Croyer's soul. He said Leslie was in a better place now, and he asked the Lord to ease the pain of his beloved Beverly. When he said this, Abigail dabbed at her eyes with a rumpled Kleenex.

Byron Summerson seemed to be holding his own, in spite of the fact I'm sure he felt as if, instead of riding the Flyer to Lock Haven, he'd climbed on a Buck Rogers spaceship and had landed on the planet Mongo. I could see he was trying as hard as he could to talk and act "straight," though that just wasn't in the cards for Summerson. I overheard one of the women remark to another that Leslie's friend Byron seemed "odd" to her. "Different" was her friend's word.

We were back at the hotel by eight-thirty. The funeral was to be at ten in the morning at the Hoster Funeral Home, three blocks away. Some people were planning to meet for breakfast over on Main Street at a restaurant called Henry's Dairy Store.

Summerson needed his beauty rest, he said, and stayed in the room he and I were sharing, but "Beverly" and I walked the block over to the town's main drag to see where Leslie Croyer must have spent a lot of carefree time during his young years. For a town in the boonies, Lock Haven had a lot going on. We saw three movie theaters with people coming and going even on a Sunday night. There were restaurants, both a Woolworth's and a Newberry's, banks naturally, drugstores, an A&P, lots of clothing stores, and a couple of pool rooms.

The Roxy Theater was showing *The Two Mrs. Carrolls*, with Bogie and Barbara Stanwyck, and Abigail said, "I love Stanwyck. She can do anything. I think I can eventually make it as an actress, but I couldn't be as versatile as Stanwyck is in a million years."

"You could win an Academy Award," I said, "for playing Beverly Andrews. Not a lot of actresses could do what you've been doing today and pull it off like you have."

She shrugged. "Easy as pie. I don't break character playing Beverly because the thing of it is, we're a lot alike. I lost a boyfriend last year and it was awful. He didn't jump off a bridge; he dumped me for another girl who was faster than I was. So the emotional part of playing Beverly isn't hard at all."

I had thought all theater girls were probably fast, but my personal experience was nonexistent.

"Aren't you uncomfortable," I asked, "putting one over on the Croyers? The whole thing seems to me to be kind of nuts. These people are deaf and blind. They make Helen Keller look like Ginger Rogers. And we're playing right along."

We ambled past the State Liquor Store, socialism for the thirsty. I had brought along my own supply, and it was back at the hotel snug in my valise.

"I don't think they're all that blind," Abigail said. "They're only as blind as they want to be. If I got skunked tonight and called up the Croyers and said, hey, you're being scammed, I'm an actress pretending to be Leslie's nonexistent bride-to-be, and your son was a homosexual, you know what they'd say? They'd say, what's a homosexual? And they'd hang up. And we'd all go to the funeral tomorrow and have a good cry, and life for the Croyer family in Lock Haven, P-A, would go on. So, do I have any qualms about tricking these nice people who lost the son they had pinned so many of their hopes on? I don't at all. I am doing a kind thing that is exactly what my sweet friend Leslie would want me to do. In fact, yeah, I'm doing it for the fifty dollars, and I'm doing it for the Croyers. But mainly, Cliff, I am doing it for my sweet, sweet, dear, dear friend, Leslie Croyer."

So Abigail was only getting fifty from Summerson? What a cheapskate. Well, I was the professional, after all.

I said, "I like to think I'm a realist. It looks like you got me beat, Abigail."

"Is it being a realist to honor a friend's harmless wishes? I think it's just being a moral person."

"I guess I'm not very moral then. You're not the first person to tell me that. But this size of a lie—it seems to me there has to be something screwy with that."

"Not," she said, "if the lie lets people live their lives the only way they know how."

I thought of Amos Leary and the German Uranian who wanted to change the homo laws. "Maybe people can learn other ways to live," I managed to say.

"If they want to. If they can see any reason to. Otherwise, I really don't think so."

She had me there. Abigail was quite smart for someone her age—though I still couldn't shake the feeling that I was involved in some giant mean practical joke, and I was as mad at Leslie Croyer as I was sorry.

We strolled back over to the hotel and sat for a while on a bench out back overlooking the Susquehanna, which was taking its time moseying down toward the Chesapeake Bay. The night was as warm as the day had been hot, and there was still some faint light in the west at almost ten o'clock. A couple of boats with outboard motors putt-putted back and forth. We each had a smoke and then went inside.

Summerson was already asleep, so instead of using the room phone I went out to the phone booth in the lobby and made my long-distance call to Quakertown. Bill Lathrop told me he was extremely relieved that I had called. He said Tom Heimer had been in touch, and Heimer badly needed to talk with me face to face as soon as I got back to Philadelphia.

CHAPTER 27

Henry's Dairy Store was famous for its pies, everybody said, but for breakfast we had hash browns, bacon, and eggs any way you wanted. The place was bright and teeming, and the waitresses in their light blue uniforms moved the orders around like those circus performers who twirl plates on top of a stick. The coffee was scalding, and Summerson cooled his in his saucer. I'd have bet that's not how they normally did it in Chestnut Hill. A few people from the Fairview Street supper stopped by our booth to tell Beverly they were sorry for her loss, and she thanked them in a voice that was so quiet it was hard for people to make out her words in the restaurant hubbub. Others from the night before were chowing down, and they were already in their somber funeral outfits, as were Abigail, Summerson, and I. My prewar blue suit was snug around the middle, and I kept the jacket unbuttoned when I stood up.

We returned to the hotel, and while Summerson and Abigail went back to their rooms one last time, I sat out on a bench by the river again. In a nearby vacant lot, a bunch of neighborhood boys, age ten or eleven, were playing ball. Most of them were pretty skilled and agile, but one was a doofus. This gangly boy, taller than the others, couldn't hit and could barely catch, and he ran a bit like a girl. But he was game, and the other boys seemed to have no problem including him. Maybe they accepted him because he helped them with their homework, or he owned the bat and ball, or he darned their socks. I guessed I knew where he was headed later in life, even if he didn't yet, and I mouthed the words in his direction, *Good luck, kid.*

The funeral home was a nice old house that once must have been lived in by some of Lock Haven's upper crust, and now anybody who paid Mr. Hoster's bill could use it for entering the gates of paradise or wherever was appropriate. Not everybody who filed in could fit in the main room, so ushers herded more peripheral mourners off to side rooms fitted with loudspeakers. On the way in, everybody passed a donation box for the March of Dimes with a picture on a poster of a boy in an iron lung. Summerson, Beverly, and I all contributed.

We three were directed to seats up front with the family. Beverly was asked to sit between Flo and Charles, and she did so, with Flo clutching her hand throughout the service. The casket containing Leslie Croyer's remains was closed for reasons of "privacy," anybody who asked was told. But the box was there for all of us to gaze at as the Reverend Pilsner remembered Leslie Croyer with words that made many people nod their heads and some choke up.

A Cub Scout, a Boy Scout, a golf caddy, a whiz at both history and languages, Croyer was also a kind and helpful young man who was well-liked around town. He was also a proud member of The Gay Pretenders, the Lock Haven High School drama club, and had leading roles in a number of their productions, including *The Farmer Takes a Wife* and *Private Lives.* During his two-year tour in the armed forces, Croyer was with a company of entertainers and once performed in a skit with the actress Dorothy Lamour.

I was seated next to Summerson, and when I heard that the high school drama club was called The Gay Pretenders, I nudged his leg with my leg and made it jump.

There were Bible verses and more prayers, and then some music somebody in another room was playing on a Hammond organ. I didn't recognize the songs—hymns, I guessed—but if you had to pick the longest distance from a Monday night jam session at Minton's to someplace else, this was it.

Ushers with white carnations in their buttonholes led us slowly out, family first, and that included Beverly, Summerson, and me. The three of us were invited for lunch on Fairview Street before our 2:48 train back to Philly, and the Croyers insisted on shepherding us around.

As we were being escorted to our ride, one of the mourners who had been seated off in a side room approached me and asked if I was Clifford Waterman. She was a tiny, late middle-aged woman with bright blue eyes, a small hat with a big feather on it, and an expressive face I instantly liked looking at. She was done to the nines like all the other "girls," as they called each other, though instead of high heels this woman wore flat shoes.

"Could I possibly talk with you for a few minutes, Mr. Waterman?" she asked. "I don't want to keep you, but I'm in charge of the drama club at the high school, and Leslie was one of my favorite students. I have friends in Philadelphia, so I've been able to follow Leslie's life there, and I can't begin to tell you how deeply sorry I am for what happened with him. It's all just so pathetically unnecessary."

Doris Gaston was her name, she said, and she offered to give me a lift to the Croyers' if we could only take ten minutes and sit and chat on the front porch of her friend Irene Planky, who lived next door to the funeral home. When I told Charles and Flo I'd catch up with them shortly, I thought they looked a little squinty-eyed when they saw who I was with, but I could have been imagining that.

"I hope," Mrs. Gaston said, lighting a Chesterfield as soon as we were seated on a couple of wicker chairs, "that I can be forward with you. It's just the way I am. It drives Dayton

Flemmspinne, our school principal, crazy."

"I like forward," I said, gratefully retrieving a Lucky from my shirt pocket. "I'm normally that way myself."

"Good. I know you are homosexual, and I know Leslie was homosexual. I knew that about him before he did, but of course I would never in a million years have said anything."

"You say you have friends in Philly."

"Theater people. I was there for ten years myself before I married Mr. Gaston and came back to introduce Noel Coward to the Susquehanna Valley. So I'm used to the ways of artistic people."

"Is the high school drama club really called The Gay Pretenders?"

She laughed. "That goes back to the twenties, as far as I can tell. I don't know if someone was being droll or just uninformed. Anyway, nobody here thinks anything of it."

"So you know about Leslie's cause of death. Not accidental drowning. Not polio."

"Oh my, if only I could have been there and talked to him!" she said, her eyes shining. "He looked up to me. He knew I was very fond of him and I appreciated his talent. And maybe later on he guessed that I guessed he was gay and that it was all right with me. I don't know. I'll never know. The idea that Leslie would kill himself to keep people in Lock Haven from knowing he was homosexual breaks my heart to pieces."

"That's what I think, Mrs. Gaston. There had to be another way."

"Yes and no," she said, and shot a cloud of smoke in the direction of the funeral home. "Growing up here, all the lessons Leslie learned about homosexuality were bad ones. As in, when he was in tenth grade, two boys were caught by the family of one of them in a sexual situation. The boys were both sent away. What did that mean—*sent away*? I couldn't begin to tell you. It's just the phrase that went around at the time, *sent away*.

Everybody whispered it, shhh, hush hush, sent away!

"Two other boys, both of them seniors at the Catholic high school, were caught the same way. One of them disappeared for six months, and when he finally came back he was wearing—guess what?—a clerical collar! A seminarian, Brother Paulie! The other one joined the Navy, I heard. The point is, to be gay was to be utterly unwelcome in this supposedly civilized little bump in the road. To some people, death must have seemed preferable to being a leper like that."

I wasn't so sure. "Yeah, well. Growing up secretly gay in a small town and then moving to a city—people do it all the time. If it's a guy, back in East Jesus the family mostly just says, oh, he's a perennial bachelor."

She rolled her eyes. "You've met the Croyers. I mean—*polio*, for heaven's sake!"

"No, boys kissing boys won't work with them."

"I heard," she said, "about the extortion being carried out by a certain Philadelphia judge and how Leslie's being a victim of this despicable reprobate is what led to his suicide. I also heard that you were doing your level best, Mr. Waterman, to do everything within your power to put a stop to this appalling state of affairs. I wanted to congratulate you, and urge you on, and to wish you every success with your admirable, critically important, moral effort to save the lives of people like Leslie Croyer. I salute you, and I thank you from the bottom of my heart."

Her eyes were glistening. I checked my watch. I said I would try.

CHAPTER 28

Mrs. Gaston gave me the name of the Philly friend who had filled her in on Leslie Croyer's life and death, David Priestly, and she said she hoped I would look him up. She said Priestly could tell me all about the likable Leslie Croyer he knew who was part of a lively group of eager young aspiring actors and actresses.

I supposed I should talk with the guy. My only face-to-face contact with Croyer had been when I struck out with Ray Phipps and The Hat and made Croyer yell at me about Gertrude Lawrence shitting scrapple on stage—not the young fellow at his most appealing. Listening to nice things someone was saying about him was the least I could do.

That was the least, the *most* being singlehandedly reforming the corrupt courts of the city of Philadelphia, which Doris Gaston, plus I didn't know how many other people, had decided was what I was going to be doing in my spare time.

How in the name of Jesus H. Christ had I ever gotten into this? I tried to remember. There were the raids by the cops at Stem t' Stern and Polly Wolly's, and then—oh, yeah—I did a little checking, and then my office burned down. Clear as a bell. So, now what? Well, I'd talk to Tom Heimer and find out what he was up to, and then we would see what we would see. Meanwhile, climbing back on that train heading downstate seemed like a great idea of a first step.

Summerson, Beverly, and I had our lunch with the Croyer family and looked at family pictures. We saw Leslie as a tot with Charles and Flo on either side of him grinning, the extended Croyer-Hoolihan clan at a cabin they rented one summer up Pine Creek, Leslie's high school graduation, Leslie in uniform onstage with Dorothy Lamour.

For the first time during our Lock Haven visit, Abigail was starting to seem less certain of how to respond. The Croyers were talking about having her visit Lock Haven again, and maybe Charles and Flo would take the Flyer down and they would all take in a Phils game together sometime.

When they asked for Beverly's address and phone number, she said she was in the process of moving and she would send her information in a few days. But then what? Nobody seemed to have thought of any of this. I was guessing that although they didn't know it, Charles and Flo had yet more heartbreak in store.

The Flyer was running twenty minutes late that day, so at the station there was an awkward period of good-byes, and then good-byes again, and then a third time before the train we heard coming around the bend from the western end of town turned out to be a long slow freight. When our train finally chugged up to where we were standing and came to a hissing halt, everybody was relieved, though Flo suddenly began to sob all over again. Beverly hugged her tightly and gave her a tissue.

"We're going to pray for you every day," Flo snuffled to Beverly.

Charles added, "We certainly are. We're going to pray for you, and Flo and I want you to know that we talked it over, and we want to tell you something. You are a young woman with your life ahead of you, Beverly. And if you"—now Charles choked up, too—"my dear, if you meet another nice young man, well—" Then he began to weep.

By now Abigail was crying real tears, and I supposed they

were partly tears of relief—a way out!—until Flo added, "And you know, Beverly, Charles and I would even . . . we would even come to the wedding!"

Every one of us was wet-eyed now, but when the conductor called "all aboard," three of us rubbed our tears away and climbed quickly up the stairs and into the coach.

I took note of the fact that the smoker was the next car forward, and I guessed Abigail was happy to see this, too.

Through the windows we could see the Croyers standing and holding onto each other with one arm and waving at the train with the other.

When we were seated and the Flyer was already passing the Piper Cub factory and picking up speed, I brought out the Jim Beam. I had swiped some Dixie cups from the Fallon House, and we all had a shot, even normally abstemious Byron Summerson, who after a few minutes asked for seconds.

CHAPTER 29

Tom Heimer was dead.

Bill Lathrop met the train at Broad Street Station when we got in at 7:35 and gave me the news. He said he had tried to reach me at the Fallon House, but I had already checked out, and the desk clerk told Lathrop I was taking the train to Philadelphia.

Lathrop said he'd heard about Heimer on the radio, the noon news reporting that a man's body had washed up in the Delaware near Chester early that morning. Police said the deceased had been identified as Thomas Heimer, a Philadelphia public school industrial arts teacher who had recently been arrested on a morals charge. Suicide was suspected because of the arrest, a possible copycat of another recent death, the suicide of an insurance company employee who had jumped from the Camden bridge after being picked up in a police sweep of sexual deviants.

Summerson and Abigail were stunned, and Abigail asked me if Heimer had been a good friend of mine. I said no, we hadn't actually met but I was maybe going to help Heimer out with a project he was working on.

"What kind of project?"

"A type of social reform."

"Good for you."

"It was a bit pie-in-the-sky."

"Are you still going to work on it?"

"Probably not. Heimer was the main impetus, and he was the one who had the wherewithal to carry the project forward."

Lathrop gave me a look. There was plainly a lot he wasn't telling me, and I was sure I knew what part of what he wasn't telling me was. Suicide? Nuh uh.

Outside the station, on fuming Broad Street, Summerson and Abigail prepared to peel off and take buses, or a trolley in her case, to where they lived. First, though, Summerson thanked the two of us profusely, and then he handed each of us a small pale blue envelope—scented, I think—containing our cash payments. We all said we would stay in touch, though that struck me as a remote possibility and we all knew it.

After they left, Lathrop said, "Where can we talk?"

"We can go to my place on Locust."

"It might not be a good idea for you to go there."

"Oh? Let me make a call."

We stopped at a cigar store to use the pay phone. A radio was playing the Benny Goodman quartet doing "Moonglow," which reminded me I was going to check with Dale Rowles to see what he'd learned about Ray Phipps and The Hat. Meanwhile, though, I found out the room at the Spruce Street rooming house was available, so Lathrop and I hiked over there. I was dragging my valise and had tossed the jacket to my good suit over my shoulder. It was stinking hot. I looked forward to maybe filching one of Bobby Carletti's cold brews in the rooming house fridge.

As we walked, while looking straight ahead Lathrop said, "I think maybe our lives are in danger."

"Both of us?"

"Somebody knows how deeply involved you are."

"Deeply involved in what?"

"What Tom was working on. Neutralizing Ray Phipps and The Hat."

Lathrop was looking less agricultural than on the day the previous week when I saw him on his farm. He was in nice dark slacks, a silky kind of white shirt, and there was no corn silk in his wavy blond hair.

I said, "I'd fight back against this thing, but I don't know what this *thing* is. What am I not understanding here, Bill?"

"I think we'll both know in a day or two. Before Tom was killed—you do understand that that is almost certainly what has happened, don't you?—before they got to him, he phoned me Sunday night from Doylestown and said he had mailed some material to me, put a lot of stamps on it and stuck it in the slot at the Doylestown Post Office. And if anything happened to him, he said that's when I should open this mail. And then I could either take action myself or, if I didn't want to get involved, turn the information over to you. He said you would know what to do."

I almost laughed. "Really? I don't know whether I'm more flattered or pissed off."

"Tom said you had a reputation for putting up with a lot of bullshit, but only up to a point. He thought you'd get to that point when you saw what he'd turned up."

"That reputation, if it's true, is only partly right. I do put up with a lot of bullshit. And then I put up with a lot more bullshit. And then I frequently put up with a good deal more bullshit on top of all the other bullshit. You can call all that putting-up-with being a sniveling chickenshit asshole if you want to, or you can call it survival. Either way, here I am and here I plan to stay."

We reached the rooming house. Lathrop stopped on the front stoop, gave me a hard look, and asked me, "So you'd even put up with murder?" His voice cracked a little as he went on. "We both know that Tom Heimer did not jump off any bridge; he was thrown. Are you going to pretend you had nothing to do with that? Really? That's not the type of person I heard you were, Clifford."

"Well, I *didn't* have anything to do with Heimer's murder, if that's what it was. Look, I am so sorry you lost your friend. He sounded like an admirable guy in a lot of ways. And I'm as curious as anybody about what Heimer might have dug up on Ray Phipps and The Hat. But I'm one little aging queer against I don't know who or what. All I know is the who or what seem to be a lot like the US Army, big and stupid and mean. It doesn't pay to fuck with them because they will eat you alive."

"Then you better take out a full-page ad in the *Inquirer* explaining all that," Lathrop said, "because who or what, as you call them, have an entirely different impression of you. Look, the building with your office in it was torched. Doesn't *that* tell you more than you need to know about where you already stand in this thing, whether you like it or not?"

I turned and led the way up the stairs to stifling room seven. I opened the window and turned both fans on. The oscillating fan kept checking Lathrop out: *Who's this guy?* I grabbed two Carlings out of the fridge. I would have to reimburse Bobby Carletti. Lathrop drank one. I pressed the other cold beer bottle against the side of my neck while I enjoyed some of the Jim Beam. We both had a smoke.

I said, "Do you own a weapon?"

"There's a shotgun at the farm that somebody must have used for hunting quail or something way back when."

"Can you use it? Not that it will do you much good."

"I've never even touched a gun."

"Not even under the auspices of Uncle Sam?"

"I was too old to be drafted. Anyway, I'd have been a CO."

"Oh. Well. It looks like you're not one anymore."

He gave a little head toss that I figured probably meant a large number of things.

CHAPTER 30

I said we'd have to take a chance and show up at my apartment, on account of that's where I kept a firearm. Anyway, I wanted to hang my suit up. It was possible there would be other funerals coming up—my own or others'—that I'd want to look nice at.

As we were on our way over to Locust Street, I asked Lathrop, "Why Doylestown? Did Heimer say anything about what he'd been doing there?"

Doylestown was a quiet, pretty little burg over in Bucks County, actually between Philly and Lathrop's farm in Quakertown. It was where James Michener the author and the songwriter Oscar Hammerstein lived. People there lived in quaint old houses and ate boiled chicken and drank gin with cranberry juice.

"There was somebody who lived there who Heimer said was going to give him some crucial information. That's all I know. He was going to explain it all when we saw each other again. But then, like I told you, he called back and said he'd mailed what it was I would need to know. And to open it if anything happened to him."

Lathrop looked over his shoulder a number of times as we walked, and then I started doing it, too. I didn't know who or what I was keeping an eye out for, and I figured neither did Lathrop.

We made it over to my building without being grabbed. In my mailbox there was a note, in addition to a sinister envelope from Bell Telephone of Pennsylvania. The handwritten note had a PPD letterhead and was from a police detective named Russell Nye. He said he was investigating the Cuthbert Street arson and would like to speak with me about any information I might have that could be helpful in his investigation. He left his number and said call ASAP.

I had left the windows in my apartment open a crack, but the place still felt like the inside of an army Quonset hut in Egypt at three in the afternoon. I got a fan whirring and opened two windows as wide as they would go. I hung up my suit. Lathrop fidgeted and looked at a week-old *Inquirer*. I saw him reading *Prober Slugs Padway at Congressional Quiz on Hollywood Unions.*

I got out my snub-nosed .38 and placed it in my valise, taking out my dirty Lock Haven clothes and putting some clean items in.

I was about to call the police dick back when the phone rang.

"I called earlier," Trevor Dunlap said, "but you weren't back yet from being out of town. I don't know if you've heard the tragic news about my roommate. Have you?"

"I heard he died, yeah. I'm sorry, Trevor. And I'm very sorry I didn't get to him earlier. They're saying Heimer killed himself, jumped off the Delaware bridge like Leslie Croyer. That's terrible. I was never able to determine where he disappeared to. Did you ever figure it out?"

"I never did. I was counting on you."

"And he never got in touch?" I asked.

"I had no idea what could possibly have become of Tom. I knew he was despondent, but it never occurred to me that he might take his own life. He never seemed the type."

"Well, often people don't seem the type until they do."

"And he didn't leave a note or anything. I checked the

apartment, but there was no sign of anything he was thinking."

As usual, I did not believe a word Dunlap was saying to me. Could it be he was even part of whoever or whatever it was that tossed Heimer off the bridge?

I asked Dunlap if Heimer's family had been in touch, and he said Heimer's brother had called, and the family back in Lancaster was stunned and distraught. The brother kept saying how surprised he was that Tom had killed himself, and asking if there was something going on with Tom the family didn't know about. Dunlap told him about the gay bar raid and the way Tom expected the school department to react if this came out.

"How thoughtful of you, Trevor, to clear things up that way."

"Under the circumstances, what would you have said, Clifford? I know his family knew all about Tom. Anyway, as a practical matter, you are now out of it. And you are off the hook. I don't suppose there's any chance of getting my ninety dollars back, is there?"

I had to say the guy had balls. "No, you were paying me to do my best, and that's what I did." So stick it in your left nostril, Mister Federal Agent.

"You were out of town. Were you looking for Tom in some other place you thought he might have gone to?"

"I was upstate at Leslie Croyer's funeral. His family is devastated, as you can imagine."

"Oh, so you weren't trying all weekend to locate Tom?"

"I did try to chase down some leads on the phone before I left town. Anyway, if it's your money you're worried about, Trevor, I should point out that you paid me for two days, Thursday and Friday. I was upstate Sunday and Monday on somebody else's dime. Let's be clear."

"I wasn't insinuating anything. Don't get me wrong. Who is your other client, if I may inquire?"

"You may not." If he really was some kind of federal snoop, he was clumsy at it.

I soon pried myself loose from Dunlap—was I rid of him forever or not?—and asked Lathrop what he knew about Heimer's roommate.

"Tom didn't trust Dunlap," Lathrop said, "and was actually planning to move out as soon as he dealt with The Hat/Phipps situation. One thing that made Tom suspicious was that Dunlap said he was homosexual, but there was no evidence he actually was—boyfriends, bringing tricks back to the apartment, dirty pictures, anything. So why was he pretending that way?"

This jibed with what Monnie Hinkle had told me. I said, "If Dunlap is a fed, it sounds like whatever he was up to was political. I'm told Tom was a big lefty—loved Norman Thomas and W.E.B. DuBois and other left-wingers. So is it possible," I asked, "that Tom was killed for political reasons? And that Trevor Dunlap had something to do with it?"

Lathrop thought about this. He was sweating in the sweltering prison of my small living room. He got some relief from the fan, but the thing was merely blowing steamy air around. A couple of times the fan blew the ash off the end of the Lucky I was smoking. It would have been a job for my cleaning lady if I had had one.

"I don't think the US government murders socialists," Lathrop said. "It tries to get us fired from our jobs, and sometimes it finds a way to throw us in jail. But shove people off bridges? That would be a whole new wrinkle. Anyway, Tom was no Stalinist. He was a union guy, and for civil rights for Negroes—like myself, and I am guessing you too, Clifford."

"Uh huh. Well, anyway, I'm voting for Truman. He's for the ordinary Joe, and I'm glad he used the bomb to end the war. And he's for the colored people, too, which gets him my vote right there."

Lathrop made a face. "Black yes, yellow no."

"What do you mean?"

"Truman is for Negro civil rights, but he didn't give a ho-hum about incinerating a quarter of a million innocent Japanese civilians when we dropped the two bombs. That was completely unnecessary. Japan was already on the verge of surrendering."

Here was a guy who didn't enlist, who was too old for the draft, and if he had been called up would have been a conscientious objector sitting in jail in Kansas rolling bandages for a couple of years. In no way would he have been a participant in a bloody invasion of Japan by US forces. So maybe on the topic of the A-bomb it would have been better for Lathrop to just keep his mouth shut.

I didn't say any of that, though. When Lathrop mentioned the atomic bomb, it reminded me of something. I told him we'd talk later about the war, but I needed to make a couple of calls. There was the arson investigator, but first I wanted to talk to Monnie Hinkle.

I got no answer at Monnie's Philly number, and then I remembered that on Monday nights he mostly took the train up to New York for the bebop jam session at Minton's. Taking a chance, I got long distance and placed a person-to-person call to Montrose Hinkle Jr. at Minton's Playhouse jazz club on West 118th Street in New York City.

It only took about five minutes—Bell Telephone of Pennsylvania was not yet ready to declare me incommunicado—but then all of a sudden, with a lot of racket in the background, there was his voice. Monnie said he had heard about Tom Heimer's suicide and he said he was pretty upset about it. But there was nothing he could do, and he thought playing his instrument would make him feel a little better, at least for the time being. So he went ahead with his Monday night gig.

Monnie didn't know that Heimer's death might have been anything other than suicide, and I didn't tell him. Why get him involved in any way?

But I did ask him, "Do you know, by any chance, if Tom knew people over in Doylestown?"

"Oh, right," he said after a moment. "I forgot about this guy. There was Tom's old pal Lucas Quayle."

Quayle. The name rang a distant bell.

CHAPTER 31

Monnie told me Heimer and Lucas Quayle had been roommates at Bucknell. They slept together back then and fooled around when they were drunk, but Heimer stayed gay and Quayle didn't—or said he didn't and anyway got married and had kids. They remained friends, even though Quayle was a stockbroker and their politics were different. Monnie said Quayle told Heimer one time, kind of joking, that maybe someday they'd get sloshed together again and see what happened.

Charleen Backus had told me that Judge Stetson had married an Elkins Park debutante named Mae Quayle and she thought they were still a married couple. I asked Monnie if he knew whether Lucas Quayle might be related to The Hat's wife, formerly a Quayle, but he said he didn't know, that Heimer had never mentioned anything about that.

Monnie and I talked about getting together sometime later in the week. He had this new Thelonious Monk record he wanted to play for me. I said I'd give him a call, though I was working on something tricky that I thought might take a while to get a handle on.

So, *was* I working on some *thing?* I talked like it, and I acted like it, so I guessed I was.

I tried calling the police dick on the arson case, but he was gone for the night and I was told to call back in the morning.

I phoned a few other people to find out whether there had been any more bar raids or other make-some-homos-jump-in-the-river incidents. There'd been a few episodes in city parks—the vice squad on the rampage—what some gays called PWB busts, arrests carried out by Perverts With Badges. There had been no bar raids over the weekend, and anyway they would not have been lucrative for The Hat, because, I was told, hardly anybody was going out.

When I offered to drive Lathrop back up to Quakertown and stay over until the mail arrived on Tuesday morning, he was grateful. I was making myself available in case either of my prime skills was called for—parallel parking and the other one—and also I had a gun. Plus, of course, maybe we would both finally find out what serious dirt Tom Heimer had on Stetson, and we could decide what to do with it. I was doubtful if it was the bomb Heimer claimed it was, but at least I'd know and could make decisions based on facts. Was getting into the thick of this whatever-it-was with Bill Lathrop, the commie corn-and-potato farmer, worth risking my life over? Apparently it was. Uncle Grant liked to say curiosity killed the cat, but that never made any sense to me.

Lathrop had taken a train into the city, and he was glad to get a ride back to Quakertown, even in my beat-up old Plymouth with its blisters and dents. It was a good *hey look I'm riding with the proletariat* car. When we climbed into the thing out behind Sal's, Lathrop probably thought he was in *The Grapes of Wrath*.

We both kept checking to see if maybe we were being followed, but I wasn't much good at that type of thing. Traffic was normal for a Monday night. We had the windows down, and the night air felt good. I had a smoke, and I couldn't wait to get to the farm and have a nip.

We stopped at an all-night diner on 202 near Doylestown and had a burger and milkshake. I hadn't eaten since lunch at the

Croyers in Lock Haven, which felt like about twenty-five years ago. I wondered if Flo and Charlie were still standing by the railroad tracks weeping, and clutching each other, and thinking about what might be a nice wedding gift for Beverly.

Then I thought, *And who exactly is responsible for all the looniness I witnessed in Lock Haven, and all the sad and ridiculous pain and suffering? Judge Stetson, The Hat, that's who.* I could hardly wait to go to bed at Lathrop's farm and sleep as soundly as I could, and then get up in the morning and wait for the mail.

CHAPTER 32

Lathrop said the mail was usually dropped off at his roadside mailbox a little after eleven. We had picked up his old jalopy of a pickup truck the night before at the Reading Line train station where he'd left it, so first thing in the morning he drove into town with four bushel baskets of corn he'd picked just after dawn. The socialist farm, as it was known locally, grew corn that was especially sweet—not a thing the Russkies would ever be able to claim—and a grocery store in Quakertown sold all the Lathrop ears they could get hold of.

After Lathrop left on his errand, I phoned Detective Russell Nye, the arson investigator. He sounded reasonable enough for about twenty seconds as he asked the initial question I would have asked if I had been able to remain on the force.

"You're a private investigator, I understand. Is that correct?"

"I am. Previously I was a detective in your department, then an MP during the war, and now I'm solo."

"Yeah, I heard about you. I might even remember you. You got booted out of the army for screwing an Arab who didn't have a pussy, just a butthole. Then the department wouldn't take you back. Is that you?"

"It wasn't just any Arab. It was the guy who kept our shower and toilet facilities almost spotless. Idriss was popular around the base. Anyway, I wasn't screwing him. He was screwing *me* at the moment somebody who thinks like you walked in. It was not just embarrassing; it nearly fucking ruined my life. Want to hear more about it?"

I could hear the metal clunk of his cigarette lighter closing. "No, I don't think I do. We all get what we deserve sooner or later."

"You're obviously still waiting, but go on."

He puffed on his—stogie? "The fire marshal has determined that the building with your office on the fourth floor was torched at about ten o'clock Friday night. An accelerant was employed to ignite the rear stairwell. Where were you at the time?"

"In a barroom."

"Which one?"

"It could have been any, I'm not sure." I didn't want this guy pestering Sal.

"A bar that caters to homosexuals?"

"That's a safe bet."

"If it was a homo bar south of Arch Street and west of Broad Street, like in that neighborhood by the railroad with all the undesirables, enjoy it while you can. That's all I can say."

"Is that a threat or an announcement?"

"What I hear, it's just a fact of life. So, if you're a private shamus, there must be a lot of people who hate your guts. Not just because you like boys, but because you're always getting into people's messes. Any of those folks that come to mind who hate you enough to maybe burn your office down?"

In fact, there were a few—or ten or twelve—but I was all but certain none of these disgruntled far-from-friends of former clients had anything to do with the fire.

I said, "There's nobody recently I can think of who's that mad at me."

"I'd love to have a look at your files."

"So would I."

"They burned up in the fire?"

"You saw what was left of the back of the building. That's where my office was."

"You didn't keep duplicate files?"

"There was a shortage of carbon paper. I guess all the carbon paper was sent to the troops. Though we didn't see much of it in Egypt."

He puffed on something again. "You have an attitude."

"Thank you."

"I don't like it."

"Having an attitude is one of my main skills. Want to hear what the other two are?"

"No, I don't."

"Then this is your lucky day."

Detective Nye asked me a few other questions that weren't especially useful or relevant, and then I asked one of him. "Any idea why the city's homosexuals are being hounded by Judge Stetson and by the police department? There's a big hike in bar raids and other anti-fairy activities, and The Hat is charging people extortionate fees to get their cases expunged. What's going on? You alluded to these goings-on yourself two minutes ago."

"All's I know," he said, "is what somebody up there somewhere wants. Maybe it's the mayor. Maybe it's J. Edgar Hoover. Maybe it's the fookin' Pope. But I can tell you this, Mr. Gumshoe-sissy-fag. If you and your people know what's good for you, you'll all move up to Satan's back porch, Greenwich Village, and leave Philly to the normal Christian folk. I just heard when I came in today that the two fairy bars on Cuthbert Street that got fumigated by the department last week are gonna be closing down for good. So you all can take it from there. It's up to you if you want to live in sexual deviate heaven or sexual deviate hell. Me, I just want to know who set that building on fire. If you get any ideas—which you, being a dumb homo prick, won't—give

137

me a call. Have a good day."

After I hung up, I wondered if changing my Yellow Pages listing to *Mr. Gumshoe-sissy-fag* would hurt business or help it.

CHAPTER 33

Lathrop didn't come back from town until about just after ten, and I was starting to worry. When he finally showed up, he said he had to pick up bread and butter and a few other necessities and that's how come he was delayed.

While we waited for the mail carrier to arrive, we sat out on the front porch and shot the breeze. Lathrop asked me about my army experience, and I told him the whole ridiculous Idriss tale. He commiserated. He said he'd had an off-and-on relationship with a younger guy from Quakertown that might have gone somewhere, but this fellow named Boyd never made it back from Guadalcanal. Lathrop thought a dishonorable discharge was better than getting blown up on a beach in the middle of the Pacific Ocean. This was a sentiment I had heard more than once, and I had to agree.

I told him the story of my own lost love during wartime, not that the Japs had anything to do with it.

"Larry Pressler was my first real boyfriend after I came back to Philly from Millersville State and joined the police. I had to be careful, and so did he on account of he was a male nurse at a Catholic hospital, Saint Agnes. We really dug each other, and I really thought after the war we'd make our nice little homo love nest in Havertown or somewhere. Get a black lab, some

Coleman Hawkins records, and a case of Jim Beam. But luck was not on my side in that regard."

"He didn't make it back?"

"Only as far as San Diego. That's where the Navy dropped him off."

"He couldn't have kept coming east?"

"Could've but didn't. First, he called and said he wanted to take a load off and enjoy the beaches in Southern Cal for a week or so. Try to put the war behind him and act like a normal human being. I missed the guy a whole lot, but I got that. Then a week turned into two weeks. And then three. And then I got my Dear John letter, and it was so not what I ever expected that I considered hiring a handwriting expert to see if the letter was some kind of a fake, a con some crazy person was running."

He looked at me. "It sounds like you were both crushed and confused."

I tossed my cigarette butt into the front yard, and I could see Lathrop's eyes following it and guessed he was fastidious. I thought, *next time use the ashtray.*

I said, "Confused, you bet—and mad. What Larry said in his letter was he'd met a girl. A girl!"

"Uh oh."

"He said he'd never before felt the way he felt about her. Her name was Carmelita, she was a waitress in El Cajon, and she was crazy about him in a way that felt oh so great. He actually talked about getting married and having a family and having what he called a normal life. That was the word he used, *normal.* Sweet Jesus."

"This happens," Lathrop said. "Usually, it doesn't work out."

"Well, it worked out for Larry. I mean, in a way it did. After about six months of this, I wrote the asshole and wished him all the best of luck with his new life with the lovely Carmelita."

"What else were you going to do?"

"Then about a year ago, I ran into this guy Bert Ramsey

who was from Philly originally but lives in San Diego now. He said, 'oh, I ran into your old beau Larry.' I said, 'was he with his bride?'"

"Right."

"Bert gives me this funny look. He says, 'you mean Carmelita?' 'That's the one,' say I. I ask him, 'have you ever met her?' He says, 'met her? I've even sucked her dick.' That was before Larry got off the boat and claimed her for his own. Bert said this person is a really hot number, one of the most breathtakingly beautiful girls in all of San Diego—and she isn't really a girl! So, no, Bill, it wasn't the Japs or the Germans who took my lover from me. It was a woman with a dick—and, Bert seemed to feel the need to tell me, a really nice one, too."

Lathrop was shaking his head sympathetically. "Good grief, did you tell Larry what you found out?"

"I let it go. If that's what the guy wanted, I could never compete. What was I gonna do, shave the hair off my ass? No, I'd heard of women with penises, and if this is what turns somebody on, who am I? Godspeed to all concerned. But I will say, since all that, I've been a little bit reluctant to give my heart away. I mean, wouldn't you be?"

I thought Lathrop was about to start telling me his own tales about love and loss, but then we both checked our watches. And we realized at almost the same time that the mail was late.

141

CHAPTER 34

When noon rolled around with no mail, that's when Lathrop phoned the Quakertown Post Office. The line was busy for several minutes. When he finally got through, I could see Lathrop listening and then saying things like "Oh no," and "That's awful" and "Yes, I was actually expecting some important mail."

He hung up and said, "The mail car was hijacked."

"Car?"

"Mildred Hockenberry has the contract for our RFD route. About a mile out of town, she was placing mail in somebody's box when she was forced at gunpoint by two men wearing masks to get out of her car. Then one of them drove away with her vehicle and she had to use somebody's phone and call in."

"Damn."

"They found her car about a mile away, but all the remaining mail in it was gone, including mine."

My impulse was to dash into the room with my valise and retrieve my .38 and hold it in my lap.

"Did the mail lady describe the assailants?"

"I didn't ask."

"She must have been able to give a description of their car."

"I don't know. The clerk at the post office was in a hurry to get off the line."

"But the lady wasn't injured?"

"I don't think so."

"At least they didn't shoot her. Or throw her off a bridge."

"So you think it's whoever is trying to keep us from finding out what Tom had to tell us about The Hat?"

"If it's not, this has to be the biggest funny coincidence in recorded history. I mean, for chrissakes, Bill."

"I'm just trying not to be terrified," he said, plainly terrified.

"You can go ahead. This is bad."

We were seated at the kitchen table drinking coffee that packed a punch—I'd learned how to do this in Egypt—and I was smoking.

"Look, Clifford, I know what happened to Tom, and of course I know we're in danger." *We* again. "I'm just trying to keep some perspective. If they—whoever *they* are—if they were following Tom and knew he'd mailed a letter and guessed it was probably coming to me, and then they intercepted the letter . . . then they must think we don't know anything yet. So, maybe now they'll just leave us alone."

Us. "You lefties are such optimists. That is, when you're not being paranoid. But I am beginning to understand you have a lot to be paranoid about. The problem is, Bill, we do know more than I think they think we know."

"Like what?"

"Like Heimer had a friend in Doylestown where he mailed the letter from who's possibly a relative of Judge Stetson. That one actually could be a coincidence, but I'm betting not. It's also possible that this guy is in some kind of jeopardy now. I think we have to warn him of the danger he's in—if he doesn't already know, which I'll bet he does—and we have to, you know . . ."

"Right. Find out from this Quayle guy what Tom found out that's incriminating about The Hat."

"Now you're cookin' with gas."

"We really are taking some big chances pursuing all this. For a few minutes, when the mail didn't come, I have to admit I almost felt relieved. That somehow we were off the hook. That we could just let events run their course."

"Naturally, that occurred to me, too," I said. "The survival instinct is to be respected. But considering what we know that apparently nobody else is hot on the trail of, I now believe we're obliged to follow through."

He nodded and then got up to get some more Egyptian coffee. Lathrop was going to have jangly nerves every which way.

I had a lot of hesitancy, too. But I thought of poor desperate Leslie Croyer sailing off the Delaware bridge, and of sweet old Doris Gaston imploring me to settle The Hat's hash, and of Charlie and Flo standing there by the railroad tracks in Lock Haven crying and hanging onto each other for dear life. And I knew I'd have to try. I tried to think of how Uncle Grant would describe what I was about to do, and I could see him looking at me and nodding sagely: "In for a dime, Clifford, in for a dollar."

CHAPTER 35

We rode down to Doylestown in the Plymouth to have a look around. The place was bustling early on a Tuesday afternoon, but bustling in a friendly, small-town way. It felt like Lock Haven, but you had the idea maybe there was a little more dough here. Just something in the cars people were driving and the way they were dressed. Nothing showy, but in a place like Doylestown that was the point.

We found a parking space on East State Street, and I backed in in one graceful swoop, one of my famous skills. In high school, one of the few A's I got was in driver's ed.

The County movie theater was playing *Kiss of Death*, with Victor Mature, Brian Donlevy and Coleen Gray. Next door to the movie was an eatery where we dropped in for a BLT for me and a tuna salad for Lathrop and two iced teas.

I asked the waitress, who looked as if she'd been around town for a while, if she knew where Lucas Quayle's brokerage firm was, and she said sure.

"That'd be Pudlow and Quayle, around the corner on South Main. Mr. Pudlow and Mr. Quayle both eat here once or twice a week."

"Have you seen Mr. Quayle this week?"

"Not today or yesterday. Not for a while, actually. I'm

145

wondering—might he be away?"

"Well, we'll go and have a look."

We had Quayle's home address on East Court Street and his phone number from the phone book. We debated whether to call him or just show up. Calling might have spooked him, so we chose to appear in person.

Partly to see what was what, we walked around the corner to the brokerage office. I had shaved that morning and used a nice aftershave and even had a tie on when I went in. The receptionist was an older woman with each nicely dyed item of hair on her head mathematically arranged and a touch of rouge on her pleasant face. I asked if Mr. Quayle might be available. With a professional smile, she told me Mr. Quayle was away for the day, and might someone else help me?

I said no, that I was just passing through and it wasn't important. I said somebody back home in Pittsburgh told me he thought I might be related to the Quayles of Doylestown, and I was curious, asking around and trying to find out. I told her my name was Ellsworth Quayle.

"Pittsburgh? That I wouldn't know about. Now, Mr. Quayle's father lives in Elkins Park. I think the family has been there for years. But Pittsburgh? Yes, you'd have to ask Mr. Quayle himself. I'm sorry he's not in the office today."

"Oh well. Any idea when he might be back in town? Or is he here in Doylestown presently?"

Now she was looking a bit uncertain. "Well, to tell you the truth, I don't know." She looked as if thoughts were buzzing around inside her head and she didn't know quite what to make of them.

"If I'm around town tomorrow, I might pop in again. Thanks for your help, ma'am."

I left her looking disconcerted, and I wondered why.

I said to Lathrop, "Elkins Park. He's related to the Judge's wife. His aunt, maybe? His dad is Mae Stetson's brother?"

"That's a good possibility."

As we walked back towards the car, I said, "How old was Tom Heimer?"

"Forty-one, I think. We're around the same age."

"He and Lucas Quayle were roommates at Bucknell, so Quayle is probably also forty-one or thereabouts. The Hat is in his late sixties, I think, so that all pretty much adds up."

Court Street wasn't that far away, but to have the Plymouth handy in case we needed it in a hurry, we decided to drive it over there. Lathrop knew the lay of the town, more or less, so he gave me directions. The Quayle house was one of the bigger ones on the street. Others nearby were old stone jobs, like Mike Stover's except not so huge, or two-floor wooden places with a smaller slanty-walled third floor on top of the two, like Mrs. Roosevelt's hat, and with a couple of windows poking out.

Built back away from the street behind at least two acres of mowed lawn, with two sky-high oak trees on either side, the Quayle place was weathered red brick with a lot of yellow wooden trim. Its wings had wings, its porches had porches, and the windows were all shapes and sizes, some like in a church, some normal, some tiny like on a jail. It was as if seventy-five years ago the architect was a joker or a heavy drinker. We could make out a tennis court to the left rear of the property.

We glanced around Court Street. A number of cars were parked in driveways and some along the street. The only sign human activity was a burly fellow in a polo shirt across the s watering his flower bed with a hose.

Lathrop said, "That guy shouldn't be watering h under this hot sun. He's going to burn them. He shou later in the day."

I made a mental note.

We parked and walked up the brick path to be the house's main door. There was an ass chairs with cushions on the porch. A si

family-size ash tray. I did not carry my .38 with me, but I had it in the car and hoped if I needed it I'd be able to get to it in time.

I pushed the doorbell button and could hear the *ding-dong* inside. We waited, and nothing happened. I pushed it again. I rapped on the door glass. Then I rapped again. I couldn't see through the lace curtain, but right when I was about ready to give up I saw movement, and then a woman opened the door.

"Are you Bill Lathrop, Tom Heimer's friend?" she asked.

"I am. This is my friend Clifford Waterman."

"I'm sorry, but you can't come in."

She was in tennis whites but instead of holding a tennis racket she was grasping a tall glass of something with green leaves sticking out. I could tell from the look of the drink and from her breath, though she was five feet away, that the glass did not contain Ma's Old Fashion Root Beer. She was lithe and blond and, if the tightness across her forehead and around her green eyes meant anything at all, under a great deal of stress.

"If you are Mrs. Quayle," I said, charging right into my pitch, "I hope you will help Bill and me locate your husband. As you might know—if you know about Tom Heimer and what happened to him—your husband might be in danger. We think we can help."

She looked past us at the man across the street with the garden hose. She said, "You don't think it was suicide either, do you? Tom going off the Delaware bridge. Lucas didn't believe it for a minute."

"No, we don't," Lathrop said. "We have reason to believe Tom was murdered."

When he said the word, it sounded a little overly dramatic to me, but Mrs. Quayle just nodded. "Yes. I guess I have to agree. But, look. Look, the thing is—the thing is, I shouldn't be seen talking to you. The important thing right now is, did you receive the list?"

Lathrop said, "List?"

"Lucas gave Tom the list. He was going to mail it to you because he was being followed, he said, and he was afraid they were going to kidnap him and take the list and then maybe even kill him. I was incredulous at first, but Lucas thinks they're capable of almost anything, even that. And by now I'm inclined to believe him."

"Our mail truck was hijacked today and the mail was stolen," Lathrop said somberly.

"Oh God."

I said, "What was this list a list of, Mrs. Quayle? And you said *they* were following Tom. Who are *they*?"

"I don't know what's on the list. Lucas says the less I know, the safer I'll be. I know it has something to do with Lucas's Uncle Harold, the judge. You probably know what an evil person he is."

Lathrop said we did.

"Well, he's even more evil than you can possibly begin to imagine. I can't talk about that. Maybe Lucas will tell you. That will be up to him."

"Where is your husband now?" I asked.

"He's going to try to get his father to intervene in whatever is going on. This . . . *list thing*. So he's in Elkins Park, or near there somewhere. Lucas is afraid he's being followed, too. The whole thing is just—I was going to say nerve-wracking. But what it is, is *terrifying*."

I asked her if she thought she was safe here alone.

"I think so. The girls are at tennis camp. Bill actually said if I thought I needed help to call you, Mr. Lathrop. So I'm glad you showed up. But I'm not going to ask you in. I have the feeling the house is being watched. For instance, I don't know *who* that man is watering the Stephens's flower garden. I've never seen him over there before. And I know Arthur and Lauren are down at the shore for two weeks. It's possible I'm being irrational, but after what happened to Tom Heimer—I mean, God!"

We asked Mrs. Quayle—she said her name was Carolyn—to ask her husband to call Lathrop and let us know how we could help. She said she would. Probably recklessly, we said we could help with both keeping Lucas Quayle safe and doing whatever needed to be done with *the list*.

Was this *list* the great and powerful magical weapon that was supposed to bring The Hat down? Lathrop and I were both perplexed. List of *what?*

CHAPTER 36

As we were about to climb back into the Plymouth, I was tempted to walk across the street and ask the man with the garden hose—the Stephens's phlox had to be screaming for mercy by now—whether or not he was the homeowners' gardener, and if not what was he doing watering their flowers in the heat of the day? I also thought about strolling over there with my .38 and shooting the guy in the leg.

Instead, we got in the car and drove away.

Carolyn Quayle had Lathrop's phone number, and I gave her mine, too, for whenever I managed to see Locust Street again.

On the drive back to Quakertown, I couldn't tell if we were being followed. We stopped a couple of times—for gas and a cold pop, and once at a farm stand selling tomatoes—and nobody pulled in nearby and waited for us to keep moving, as far as I could tell. Though they, the mysterious *they*, knew where Lathrop lived, so *they* had no need to track our movements.

We were back in Quakertown before the post office closed, and we went inside hoping for an update on the mail-car hijacking. We walked past a couple of state troopers talking to a guy whose black shoes shone brighter than a thousand suns—a fed, I figured.

Lathrop knew the postal clerk, an older gent named Walt

with hair growing off the side of his nose. He told us the stolen mail had not been recovered, and everybody who worked at the post office felt terrible about it. Mrs. Hockenberry had described the masked robbers to the police, saying they were good-sized, had muscles, and were dark-complected but not colored. Walt said the police had learned that the car the hijackers were driving was a maroon Dodge that had been stolen from a driveway in Perkasie an hour before the unfortunate incident.

It was still hot as blazes when we got back to the farm. Lathrop had a pond out back and said, "let's have a swim and cool off." The pond was shielded from the road by some scrubby trees, and he took off all of his clothes and waded in. I noted that he was a really good-looking guy and well put together, splashing around in his birthday suit, but now was not the time to be thinking about any of that. I stripped down to my boxers—I was a Democrat but no socialist—and walked in and got wet. I had laid my .38 on top of my trousers and was never more than ten feet away from it at any one time.

Lathrop had a wooden bench next to the pond and a couple of ratty old towels, so we dried off and sat and had a smoke. I noticed that he had a kind of semi-boner, but I chose to ignore it and mine as well.

I suggested we should be near Lathrop's phone in case Lucas Quayle called—or his wife did—so we soon went inside.

Lathrop had some chores to do before it got dark. He'd been building a new shed for his old tractor and wanted to get in an hour's work on it, and he went back outside. I got into some dry underwear and sat for a while waiting for the phone to ring. When it didn't, I made a few calls I'd been putting off. I phoned a couple of Philly bar owners, Sal first, to find out out if there had been any more raids.

Sal said, "No more raids this week, but didn't you see the paper?"

"The *Inquirer*? No, I've missed a couple of days."

"Half the guys picked up at Stem and at Polly-Wolly's got their names in the paper today as perverts."

"Damn."

"It said disturbing the peace, but it said they were arrested in places frequented by sexual deviants. It gave their names and their addresses and even who they worked for. I heard about two guys who were fired already, a fourth-grade teacher and a guy who delivered laundry. People are crapping in their pants all over Center City. Nobody knows what the hell is coming down the pike next!"

I said, "These are the ones who couldn't pay."

"It looks that way."

I thought of Carolyn Quayle's remark that her husband's Uncle Harold, Judge Stetson, The Hat, was an evil man, and he was even more evil than what I already knew about him. I knew plenty, and what Sal told me next was even worse.

"I know you don't want to hear this," Sal said. "But somebody better tell you."

"Now what?"

"There were two names in the paper that shouldn't have been in there."

"*None* of the names should have been in there, but what do you mean?"

"Two of the guys who failed to pay the five hundred failed to pay on account of they were dead."

I could feel my lunch start to loosen in my stomach, and churn and rumble upward, and I struggled to keep it down as Sal recited their names.

CHAPTER 37

"It must have been a mistake," Lathrop said when I told him that Tom Heimer's and Leslie Croyer's names had been printed in the who's-a-queer report in the paper. "How could the court—and the *Inquirer*—not have known?"

"It was no mistake. They knew."

"It was just needless cruelty?"

"That and a warning."

"Who was being warned and for what possible purpose?"

We were at the kitchen table again. Lathrop had come in from his chores and uncapped a cold Schlitz, and I had helped myself to a serving of my own Jim Beam which I'd brought along.

I said, "It's more anti-homo craziness. Drive us out of that neighborhood for some unknown reason. They're telling us that they goddamn mean business. Whoever *they* are. *Hey, you pansies! You don't want your life ruined? Or brought to a premature violent finish? Then get the hell out!* And it looks like it's going to work, too. So far."

"Maybe it's the archdiocese," Lathrop said. "I know the cardinal gave a speech not long ago where he condemned the evil of sexual perversion."

"I don't know about homicide. And hijacking the US Mail? Arson? Would the church do that?"

"No, I was raised Catholic, and I remember that the priests are somewhat subtler."

"It's The Hat who must know what on earth is happening here. We're back to that. The Hat and Ray Phipps."

Then I remembered something, and while Lathrop got some supper together I called Dale Rowles to find out if he had had any luck getting any dope on Phipps or Judge Stetson. He'd said his wife had a friend who had a friend who'd had an affair with Phipps.

I reached Rowles at home, who was about to join his well-informed wife for supper, so I tried to make it quick.

"Yeah, what it is, is this: Ray Phipps is quite the skirt-chaser, I'm told," Rowles said. "Connie's friend's friend had a fling with him when she was between husbands a couple of years ago. He has a long-suffering missus at home who plays a lot of golf. But she likes their fancy digs in Wynnewood with the pool and the pool house with the well-stocked wet bar, and the winters in Miami Beach, so she puts up with Ray's extramarital shenanigans. Connie's friend's friend said she was married to the most boring man in Haverford for twelve years, and for a change of pace she was looking for something sordid, and Ray Phipps fit the bill."

"Sordid, meaning adultery?"

"Not just. Phipps had multiple bed partners at times, I mean all at once, and Connie's friend's friend sometimes joined in. She said she was shy at first, but it didn't take her long to get over her initial hesitancy."

I had heard about how there were straight people, too, who did this type of thing, but it was somewhat shocking to me and I didn't like to think about it.

"What about Judge Stetson?" I asked. "Is he a philanderer, too, or does your wife's friend's friend not have that kind of information?"

"I wouldn't know about that. I've never heard that. I know

Mrs. Stetson is considered to be a very private person. She might be religious."

"Anyway," I said, "it sounds like Phipps lives like the King of Egypt on a court clerk's salary, and his wife lives like the Queen of Sheba. Anybody have any idea how that is possible?"

"With Connie's friend's friend—who he wined and dined at all the most *cherce* Frenchified establishments—Phipps got a kick out of joking about spending all his whiny wife's family money. But Connie's friend's friend asked around, and she found out Phipps's wife was a Pontoonski from Scranton, or something like that, and the Pontoonskis didn't have a *sou*. So, where was all the money coming from? An open question."

"Yeah," I said, "open, and open to informed speculation."

I asked Rowles if he had turned up anything additional on Trevor Dunlap. On Friday he told me he'd heard Dunlap was working on some so-called special project at the mint.

"I couldn't get much on Dunlap. Sorry. It seems to be some hush-hush thing he's been assigned to, but nobody I know has any idea of what it is."

"I wish I knew what's going on with that. Dunlap might be mixed up somehow in The Hat/Phipps criminality, but I can't seem to puzzle out how."

"It sounds, Clifford, as if you're bent on fixing Phipps's wagon, and of course Judge Stetson's. All I can say is, good luck with that holy crusade. Be careful not to get your saber bent."

I asked Rowles if he had heard about Tom Heimer's suicide, and he said he had, and wasn't that sad and terrible?

I said, "It's worse than sad and terrible. There's plenty of evidence I've turned up that Heimer was abducted and thrown off the Delaware bridge. He had something on Judge Stetson, and I am now in the process of trying to discover what that incriminating thing is. It's not just blackmail and extortion. Everybody in Philadelphia seems to know about that stuff, and ho-hum. A man related to the judge who I'll soon be in touch with claims it's something even worse. So, stay tuned, Dale."

There was a long silence before Rowles finally said, "Are you sure you want to be involved in this?"

"To tell you the truth, I don't. I'm afraid I might end up in the river. Or like some guy in Germany a long time ago in the insane asylum. But I am pissed off enough at these gangsters that I'm going to see what I can maybe get away with. So, wish me luck."

After a moment, Rowles said, "Oh, I do. I do wish you all the luck in the world."

Lathrop had grilled two steaks, medium-well for me, rare for the socialist. He had sliced some vine-ripened tomatoes and boiled six ears of corn for three minutes. Butter, salt, and pepper were on the table. We didn't say much while we ate, but we agreed it was one of the best meals we had ever eaten.

CHAPTER 38

While we waited to hear from Lucas Quayle—he seemed to be taking his own sweet time getting in touch—Lathrop told me more about Tom Heimer. They'd been pals since high school in Lancaster. Neither knew the other was gay back when they met, and each of them was only vaguely aware of certain alarming longings that both definitely felt were not to be talked about.

They were both readers and interested in history. Revolutions were exciting, especially the American one, the French, and the Russian. They loved reading about people overthrowing tyrants, types of people like their asshole high school principal, Hiram C. Plessinger. For one school talent show, the two boys did a skit where President Coolidge was portrayed as a quacking duck wearing a top hat with a big dollar sign on it. Hardly anybody at the school thought this was funny, except for a few teachers.

After high school, the two young men went their separate ways—Tom to Bucknell and Bill off to the ag school at Penn State—but they had stayed in touch. When they were both thirty years old and having one of their periodic get-togethers, Tom tremblingly admitted—he was terrified that the news would destroy their friendship—that he was homosexual. Bill then blurted out, "Oh, me too!" They did not become lovers. Their relationship was solidly something else by that time, but the revelation deepened the friendship, and whenever one or the other needed a helping hand or a ready ear, the other man was there.

As Lathrop neared the end of telling his story of this great true friendship, his voice wavered and his eyes were wet. Up until this moment, he had seemed more frightened than bereaved when talking about Tom Heimer being murdered. But now the loss of his dear chum was getting to him in a major way. I wanted to comfort Lathrop, but I wasn't sure how. We were at the kitchen table, and I made myself put my hand over his. It felt weird—unmanly?—but he let me do it. Grabbing his dick would have felt like the most natural thing in the world. But a guy holding another guy's *hand*?

Anyway, I kept hold of Lathrop's calloused farmer's paw for a minute or two while he cried. Then I let go and offered him a cigarette, and although he had told me he hardly ever smoked, he took it.

We had a drink and listened to the Phillies game for a while—they were beating the stuffing out of the Braves up in Boston—and then some music on the radio. Lathrop didn't have any jazz and not a whole lot of any kind of records. He said Heimer liked jazz, and I said, yeah, I'd heard that from Monnie Hinkle.

Lathrop said he liked folk music best. "It often has political ramifications that I especially appreciate."

"Monnie said Tom thought Negro jazz had political ramifications too. Though the politics were more indirect."

There was no need to mention that Monnie told me Heimer liked to imagine he was being penetrated by W.E.B. DuBois.

The radio music was pretty much just background noise. Art Lund singing "Mam'selle," Freddy Martin's band doing "Managua, Nicaragua." Lathrop and I each had another drink, one for the road, the road to some shut-eye.

It was almost eleven and Lucas Quayle hadn't called. Had

he decided not to have anything to do with us? Had he joined the other side—whoever *the other side* was? Was he floating in the Delaware, and his body was going to wash up on the shore near Wilmington in the morning, his brains bashed in by some type of blunt object, maybe a baseball bat autographed by one of the Phils' stars like Eddie Waitkus?

Lathrop and I had one more smoke and sat there in the farmhouse kitchen and discussed all the reasons Quayle might not be going to call, and then at 11:10 the phone rang.

CHAPTER 39

Lathrop spoke with Quayle first. I tried to overhear what Quayle was saying but only caught a word here and there. Lathrop told Quayle about Heimer coming to him for help getting dirt on the wicked Judge Stetson and hiding out on the farm and then saying he was going off to meet somebody—"That must have been you, Lucas"—and then never coming back and turning up dead in the river. He told Quayle that before his body was found, I had shown up at the farm looking for Heimer. He said I had been directed there by a man named Trevor Dunlap, Heimer's roommate, who supposedly worked in security at the mint.

This time I could make out Quayle saying loudly, "Oh no, not that guy!"

It sounded as if, as I had suspected, Dunlap was either using me to try to track down Heimer, or Dunlap and whoever he was working for wanted all of the troublemakers, including Quayle, to be brought together in one place in order to deal with us as *they*—whoever *they* were—saw fit.

Quayle asked to talk to me, and Lathrop handed me the receiver. I had lit a cigarette and it smoldered away in an ashtray. A warm breeze had kicked up outside, and it blew in the kitchen window next to us and through the house and out through the front screen door.

"My wife told me you were a private investigator who was willing to help us out," Quayle said, "and, believe me, I appreciate the offer very much. You realize, of course, that what we're all trying to do is very dangerous."

"Well, yeah. I mean, they killed Tom Heimer for goodness sakes. Whoever *they* are. It's plain they're ruthless, and that is why at this very moment I am sitting at Bill Lathrop's kitchen table with a loaded thirty-eight-caliber revolver within easy reach."

"I've got a gun, too," Quayle said. "I've never shot one of these things in my life. This one belonged to my wife's mother. It's a small derringer she carried in her reticule whenever she went into the city from Elkins Park to shop at Wanamaker's or Gimbel's. I think it's loaded, but I'm not sure. Maybe you can show me how to use it."

In one way, this was good. It meant I would meet Quayle soon. Also, a *reticule*—pocketbook of some kind?

"Sure," I said, "I'll show you how it works. Look, it sounds like after Heimer met you in Doylestown over the weekend and retrieved the incriminating evidence on Judge Stetson, he realized he was being followed. He must have been seen going into the Doylestown Post Office, buying a stamped envelope, and mailing whatever it was to Bill. Then he was grabbed and taken away, and that was the end of that poor guy. You probably know that Bill's mail was hijacked today, so he never received whatever this damning information is. Speaking of which, what the hell is it?"

Quayle sighed. "Oh God. Well, it's complicated. We should meet, and I can explain it all. It will take considerable explaining. When might you be available to get together with me in Elkins Park?"

"As soon as you like. But for chrissakes, give me a hint as to what's going on here that involves suicide, and arson, and murder, and I'm betting plenty more. Something about a so-called *list*. Your wife told Bill and me that Judge Stetson—The Hat, as he's known in Philly—is actually more evil than we can even begin to imagine. What does that mean? Is his body inhabited by Satan?"

"Is Carolyn all right?" he asked anxiously.

"She was a little green around the gills when we saw her, but uninjured."

"She told me she's coping, and the girls are away at tennis camp. I don't think they'll go after her," he said, as if to reassure himself. "It's me they're worried about, and they are right to worry. I *am* trying to sort this whole thing out without any further violence, but families can be complicated, as I'm sure you understand. Anyway, I'll explain it all when I see you. In the meantime, I can tell you it's about a family situation and also—a really big *also*—it's about money. I mean, more money than you or I would ordinarily conceive of in our wildest imaginings."

"I charge forty-five dollars a day. So, I think you've got me on that one."

"It's also about history," Quayle added. "That's why so much is at stake."

"History, eh? Do you mean George Washington history? Benjamin Franklin? Archduke Ferdinand? Toss me a bone here, Lucas."

"No, it's more recent history. When I explain, you'll understand right away. Bill said you got involved in this situation when Trevor Dunlap hired you to locate Tom. But you can't trust Dunlap, I can assure you of that. Tom was sure he was FBI, but not the kind of FBI that captures bank robbers. He's political, going after communists or people J. Edgar Hoover or somebody thinks are communists. That's why he was spying on Tom, a liberal who's in a union. Tom and I have always been pretty far apart politically, but I know he's no Red."

"I know you and Tom were quite close when you were roomies at Bucknell."

He chose to let this go by—he maybe guessed what I knew or maybe he didn't—and he said, "Tom suspected that Dunlap had been recruited on top of his Red-hunting to help with the project we're all dealing with here. Do not under any circumstances trust this man or have anything more to do with him if at all possible."

I said, "Project?"

"Can you meet me at ten in the morning in Elkins Park? I'm having breakfast with my father first, and by ten o'clock I might be in a position to fill you in and tell you whether or not this entire situation can be resolved without further bloodshed."

"Sure. Where should I show up?"

He gave me the name and address of the inn where he was staying.

I asked, "Should Bill come along? He'll probably want to." Across the table from me, Lathrop looked at me for a few seconds and then gave a little nod.

"It'll be better if Bill stays on the farm. His chickens will need him."

"He doesn't have any chickens."

"Well, the potatoes. No, the thing is, from here on out, it would be better if anybody involved in this should be armed."

"You said you weren't sure how to use a firearm."

"All too true. But you said you would teach me."

I said, yeah, I supposed I had.

CHAPTER 40

Two cop cars were parked outside the Poplar House Inn when I got there at about a quarter to ten in the morning, and this was not a good sign. One vehicle was an Elkins Park cruiser, the other a statie.

It had taken a while to make it down from Quakertown in the morning traffic, but I'd left early and stopped at a place on 611 outside Elkins Park for coffee, eggs, and toast. The Plymouth was acting well-behaved, maybe because a light drizzle was drifting down for a change, instead of a blazing sun pounding the bejesus out of every object in sight.

Elkins Park was quite the spiffy little burg with a goodly number of old-money mansions either inhabited by the remnants of the families who had made a killing building modern Philly seventy-five years ago, or turned into private schools or rest homes for local oldsters missing a marble or two.

The Poplar House Inn looked as if it had been one of these upper-class places, or maybe medium-upper, as it wasn't quite as big as others on this street. The front of the house had a long face, like Miss Pergrem, my seventh-grade algebra teacher, and I hoped the place was nicer to spend time with than she had been. I didn't know if the Poplars were the family who built the house or if there had been poplar trees around it, but the trees in the

165

front yard at the present time were horse chestnut.

There was a front desk in the entry hallway, and three cops were talking with a man standing behind it. There were two troopers in addition to the local officer, and so far no sign of Lucas Quayle, even though it was a bit after ten.

The man behind the desk—seventyish, stout, with horn-rimmed glasses, and hair that looked a bit mussed—acknowledged me and said to please wait, he would be with me in just a moment.

I stood back and turned away—*dum-de-dum*—but listened while the cops asked the innkeeper questions. It soon became apparent that there had been gunfire in the inn in the middle of the night. The local cop had heard the innkeeper's story earlier, it seemed, and now the man behind the desk was repeating it for the staties. There was a bullet hole in a second-floor window frame—small-caliber, the local cop stated—and another bullet was lodged in the wall of the guest room. There was no sign of blood anywhere, and the guest in that room, a Lucas Quayle, had left the inn around the time the shots were fired.

"He didn't check out?" one of the troopers asked.

"I had been sleeping until the shots woke me up," the innkeeper said. "I didn't get out of bed immediately. By the time I got up enough nerve to come out and look around, the guest had left the inn. I checked, and his car was no longer parked back by the garage. Fortunately, he had paid in advance."

"For how many nights?" one of the staties asked.

"He arrived the day before yesterday, Monday afternoon, and paid for three nights."

I was sending thought waves over to the same trooper who asked that question, and he must have heard them. He said, "Did Mr. Quayle take his belongings with him when he left?"

"Yes, he did. As far as I can determine, nothing was left behind. His room, room three, had a private bath, and nothing was in there this morning, no toothbrush or shaving set as far as

I have been able to ascertain."

And it sounded like no *list*.

"Two of the neighbors," the local cop said, "say there were more than two shots fired. One lady says three; another guy says four."

The trooper who seemed to know what he was doing got the neighbors' names and said he would talk to them.

I had been standing back in the shadows examining some brochures about Elkins Park sights to see, and after the manager was asked what he knew about Lucas Quayle—he said, "Nothing, except he had a driver's license with a Doylestown address"—I ambled over and stood in the front doorway. I looked up at the drizzle, checked my watch, and then moseyed down the front steps and out to my car. Then I drove away.

I found a pay phone at an Atlantic station. Bill Lathrop answered right away. He said he'd been waiting anxiously for any news, and I asked him if Quayle had been in touch. He said no, and I described what I had just seen and heard.

"Oh no!"

"*Oh no* is right. Look, I'm coming back there, and I can help you keep an eye out for whatever the hell we should be keeping an eye out for. But first I want to talk to somebody here in Elkins Park. And then I'll swing by Doylestown and check on Carolyn Quayle. Maybe her husband has been in touch with her."

"God, this has to be really, really bad. Am I right?"

"Yes, Bill, bad it really, really is. Look, I would actually suggest that you leave the house and hide out somewhere, but somebody should be there to answer the phone in case Quayle or his wife calls. Can you hang on for a couple of hours until I get there?"

"Sure. I mean, why would anybody come after me since I don't really know *anything* as to what the hell is actually going on here. Do you?"

"No, but I hope to know a whole lot more in an hour or so."

CHAPTER 41

The Quayle family homestead had seen better days. Like the Poplar Inn, it was on a nice street of big old houses with a lot of lawn around them, and pink and red hollyhocks along the sides of the garages, and rose bushes or hydrangeas growing up to the railings of the front porches. But this one's walls had once been covered with wooden shingles and now some had fallen off and others were in need of a paint job. The grass could have used cutting, though the bees must have been loving all those dandelions, or would when the rain let up and the sun came back out again.

The owner of the Atlantic station where I used the pay phone knew where everybody in town lived. I didn't tell him I was Ellsworth Quayle. He looked like a guy who could spot a bullshitter, and he'd just answered my question when I asked where the Quayles lived. He also gave me Lucas Quayle's father's first name, Parsons.

"You mean Parson?"

"No, Parsons."

I knew there were types of people who used old family last names as first names, and I was glad mine was not one of those. My mother's people were Fenstamachers, and I would not have liked going around as Fenstamacher Waterman.

Parsons Quayle answered the door soon after I knocked, as if he had been expecting me, which he had.

"My son phoned earlier and said you were likely to be stopping by. Come on in and I'll fix you something."

He was as tall as I was, bony-faced and sad-eyed, freshly shaven with a speck of toilet paper stuck to his chin. He was dressed for lunch at the Cricket Club but probably wouldn't be showing up there, as his collar was frayed and his gait was that of a man whose feet were killing him. *Gout?*

I followed Mr. Quayle through a couple of heavily furnished dim rooms that smelled vaguely of something acrid, maybe the ghost of cat piss. He led me to his study, which had shelves of books that looked as if someone had read them. I saw some Ernest Hemingway. Speaking of bullshitters, there was one. Even though his really good no-fancy-pants first book contained the best line in American literature, "Isn't it pretty to think so." Back at Millersville, after I read that novel for a class, I asked Grandma Fenstamacher to tat that line on a sampler for me to hang over my couch. She said she would, though she never quite got around to it.

From a trolly cart with drinks and ice in a bucket, Mr. Quayle poured me some plain soda—"It's early yet"—and a glass for himself, and then led me through the study to a small screened-in porch that looked like his special hidey-hole, with two cushioned wicker rockers.

The warm light rain drifted down on three sides of us as Mr. Quayle lit a Chesterfield with a Ronson lighter—*click, skritch, clunk*—and I used a match on my Lucky.

"Lucas is in a lot of trouble," he said, spouting smoke, "and it worries the dickens out of me. But he's always done things his way, practically since he emerged from the womb. I just hope he manages to survive this fuss. He tells me you're going to help him, and you have my sincerest wishes for your own opportunity to continue on in this vale of tears we all seem doomed to inhabit."

With the flowery language, was he laughing at me? Or laughing at himself? The second one, I tentatively decided.

"So you spoke with Lucas on the phone. I know he meant to have breakfast with you."

"That didn't work out, as I suppose you know. You went by the Poplar?"

"Just as some cops were there talking about gunshots in the night, with bullet holes in Lucas's room, and no Lucas to be found."

"He escaped by the skin of his teeth," the old man said, shaking his head in near disbelief. "Gangsters! Lucas is being pursued by gangsters! It's why he stayed at the Poplar instead of here at the house. My late wife would never have believed in a million years it would come to something like this. I mean, Lord!"

"I am sorry for your loss. Did your wife pass away recently, Mr. Quayle?"

"Before the war. Heart condition. I've been pottering around here on my own for nigh on ten years now. Though not for much longer, I don't think. The end is near, as that useful saying goes, and I thank the good Lord for that."

"I'm sorry to hear that. Are you in ill health?"

"Not really, just foot problems. A kind of neuropathy, they call it—sick nerves. It hurts like the devil sometimes. No, I expect to live to a hundred and twelve like most of the Parsons and Quayles. It's this place that's soon to be on the auction block, not me. I'll miss it, but I can't keep it up or pay the confiscatory taxes, so I'm clearing out and investing the proceeds in the surest kind of sure thing so that I can carry on. And maybe even have something left over to leave to my grandchildren."

"Which sure-thing investment? American Tobacco? The phone company?"

He sniffed. "That's the part I'm not supposed to talk about, the nature of a particular investment. It's confidential. Lucas can tell you about it if he wants. I have advised him not to. Not yet, but he has his own way of doing things. Which you can see where that has gotten us all. I mean, gangsters! I'm still just reeling from the very idea of it."

"Where is Lucas, if I may ask? He'll probably be in touch with me, and I'm hoping to be able to meet him face to face to sort out what's going on here."

"Yes, he said he'd contact you. But where is Lucas? I haven't the faintest idea. He told me I'd be better off not knowing. Whatever that is supposed to mean. These days I just roll with the punches when it comes to my son. And those haymakers do seem to keep coming."

"Well, sir," I said, "here comes another one: Lucas has damaging information about your brother-in-law, Harold Stetson, that he believes should be publicly known. I expect you are aware that Judge Stetson is notorious in Philadelphia for extorting money from persons appearing before him in the courtroom. Especially homosexuals."

"Ah, yes, Harold and his habit of putting the squeeze on the pansies and making them go boo-hoo. Why does he do that? It's so unseemly. Why he even wants those types of individuals in his courtroom is beyond me."

"Just greed, I suppose. It's an opportunity to exploit certain social attitudes."

"Well, if some types of men feel the need to stick it in another man's back door, I say let them. I go along with the modern thinking on this one. I say live and let live. Just so they don't think *I'm* going to bend over for them. Or my son is. Anyhow, Harold is no man to judge, that's for goddamn certain!"

"Yes, Lucas mentioned to me in passing that Judge Stetson is far from perfect himself, morally speaking. What did Lucas mean by that?"

"Why, why—" The hand with his glass of soda began to shake, and he waved the glass around as he spoke. He blurted out: "He beats her! He beats my sister! He beats Mae and she puts up with it. Once he threw her down the back steps and she broke her collarbone. I have warned Harold countless times that this is not acceptable behavior, and he pays me no heed at all. That man is a son of a bitch, that's what he is! But there is not a blessed thing I can do about it. When Lucas found out, he was furious. He wanted to confront his Uncle Harold, and it was all I could do to keep him under control. All we need at this point is for us to get on the wrong side of Harold. *That*, I told Lucas, is simply not going to happen. Not that Lucas is necessarily going to listen to his old dad, Lord help us all!"

I said, "Why is it bad to get on the Judge's side *at this point*, as you just put it?"

"That is not," he said firmly, "a topic I am prepared to discuss at the present moment—if ever."

CHAPTER 42

On the way out of town, I swung by the Poplar House Inn but didn't stop. The two cop cars were still parked out front. I supposed the state troopers were looking for more bullet holes and questioning the neighbors.

Parsons Quayle had filled me in on plenty that was news to me, but the overall situation was still murky or worse. Before I left, the old man had ranted some more about his brother-in-law, The Hat. He said, yes, he had heard that term used in reference to the judge, but he didn't really clarify things well enough for me to puzzle out what was going on with murder, and arson, and all the rest of the current lethal looniness.

I asked Mr. Quayle about a list that would clarify what was happening, but that's when he pretty much clammed up. I asked him if there was a list of the times his brother-in-law had attacked Mr. Quayle's sister Mae, or a list of her injuries—he had mentioned a broken collar bone—but he had nothing to say on the subject of anything you could call a list. Anyway, without testimony from the victim, how was anyone going to hold the judge responsible for his brutality? I knew from my disreputable line of work that men beating their wives wasn't all that unusual, sad to say. And it wasn't only in low-class families where this went on, poor colored or white trash.

I thought for about two seconds that I might visit Mae Stetson and urge her to report her husband to the authorities, but naturally I knew what a fool's errand that would be. If she ignored the entreaties of her own brother to demand a stop to this behavior, she was not going to even let me past the front door. And it wasn't like with pets where if a dog was being mistreated you could call the dog officer and report the cruel owner. Wives didn't rate that highly.

So I still needed to meet Lucas Quayle face to face. It sounded as if he had survived some kind of attempt to kidnap him and then—what? Shoot him? Take him to Philly and toss him off the bridge? Or had he *not* survived the attack—despite getting a shot or two off with his wife's mother's derringer—and been forced to drive his own car to a location of the bad guys' choosing, where both Lucas and his vehicle had ended up floating in Delaware Bay? Apparently none of those bad things had befallen Quayle during the night since he had phoned his pop that morning.

But what did some kind of "investment," as Lucas's father called it, have to do with the gangsters, so-called, or any of the rest of it? As far as I knew, only Lucas had the answer to that.

I headed north and stopped at Doylestown on my way to Quakertown. The rain had pretty much let up, and breaks in the clouds here and there let some rays of sunshine pour through. At first this was a welcome sight, but as the muggy air got hotter and the Plymouth's engine began rattling, I thought, *well, here we go again.* I pulled up in front of the Lucas and Carolyn Quayle house on East Court Street just after two. The guy watering the phlox across the street was gone, but it had rained, so if he was a bad actor he would be needing some other type of cover for his surveillance in any case.

When I walked up to the big house's front door, I noted to my chagrin that it was wide open.

I walked back to the car and stuck my .38 in my belt.

Back at the front door, I did not call out but eased my way inside with my weapon now in hand. Lights were on in several rooms. In the big living room, the overhead light fixture was on. The room had a lot of furniture of the type Scandinavians like, comfortable enough but minus any doo-dads. There was a Dumont television set on a table facing a couch and two easy chairs. I wondered if the TV was picking up all three of the Philadelphia stations.

A large dining room had modern furniture, too, Palmolive-soap-colored, with modern art on the wall, like bebop you could look at. Here also the overhead light was on. In the kitchen, the refrigerator was humming away. I opened it and noted among the other normal contents a block of cheese. I hadn't had lunch, only a Hershey bar and several cigarettes in the car. I doubted if the Quayles would have minded if I swiped a chunk of cheese, but I had a gun in my hand.

I backtracked and moved into another wing of the house and a room that protruded off the side of the building that must have been Lucas Quayle's study, as it contained bookshelves and a desk. This room had been ransacked. The desk drawers were all open, and papers and files were strewn everywhere. Books had been tossed from their shelves. It appeared to be not merely a search mission, but search and destroy. The vandalism was a message.

I was fearful that I would find Lucas and Carolyn Quayle's bodies upstairs, bloodied and mangled, but I didn't. I looked all through the house but found no sign of violence to life and limb, just to things. The master bedroom had also been turned inside out, with clothing tossed all around. What were plainly the bedrooms of the Quayle daughters had not been interfered with. That they were merely normally untidy was my impression.

A good sign was that out behind the house one car was parked, a gray Buick coupe. I supposed that the Quayles owned two cars as people of their class mostly did, and one was missing.

I supposed, or hoped at least, that Lucas had picked up his wife in his car and driven her to safety somewhere before—or even after?—intruders had broken into his home. Now it was up to me to locate the two of them and finally get the lowdown on what all we were dealing with here. Large sums of money was one thing. Wife-battering another one. Investments? "History"? What else?

Now I had a list of my own.

CHAPTER 43

Lucas Quayle had not gotten in touch with Lathrop, and that was a worry. His father had said Lucas had survived his encounter with "gangsters" and he would contact me. But he hadn't, and now both Lucas and his wife were . . . *missing* was what I would definitely call it. Maybe they weren't thinking of it that way, wherever they were, but I doubted they had driven into the city to pick up shot glasses in Gimbel's basement.

Before I left Doylestown, I had dropped in at the brokerage, Pudlow and Quayle, and was told again that, so sorry, Mr. Quayle was away from the office for a few days.

Lathrop had been busying himself with his crops. He said that from the near end of his potato field he could hear the kitchen phone ringing, and he had tried to stay in range. He had, however, run a couple of bushels of corn into Quakertown midmorning, and he said it was possible Quayle had phoned during that half-hour period. Though if it was important, which we both knew it certainly would have been, Quayle would have called back.

Sitting and waiting would have driven me crazy, so while Lathrop tended to his fields and his new tractor shed, I got on the phone. I tried to keep the calls short, but I wanted to know what was going on in Hat Ground Zero while I was ka-banging around the suburbs like a ball in a pinball machine.

I had picked up an *Inquirer* in Doylestown, but there was nothing in this day's edition about additional degenerates being arrested. It was just "Bank Aide's Home Town Stunned by Huge Theft," and "New Polio Case Found in Philadelphia." I wondered how things were going up in Lock Haven and if "Beverly Andrews" had been in touch with the sad folks along the Susquehanna.

The paper also had a story on Mike Stover's wife, Gwendolyn, who had been in charge of raising half a million smackeroos for the Philadelphia Orchestra. There was a picture of her with Eugene Ormandy, and she was wearing a kind of tiara that looked like it represented an entire trainload of car and truck tires.

I tried calling a couple of bar owners, including Sal, and he was the only one I was able to reach. He told me business was terrible all over town for gay hangouts, and Stem t' Stern and Polly-Wolly's were closed temporarily and maybe even permanently.

Sal said, "Stem had some smoke damage from a fire next door the other night, so that might be part of the reason they're still closed down. I've heard four or five different stories."

"The fire was in the building next door to Stem? What building is that? I don't recall exactly."

"It had a pawn shop and a cigar store on the first floor, and upstairs I'm not sure. The building is a lot like yours that burned down, three or four floors with offices but no apartments. The place is still standing, but I guess there's a lot of smoke and water damage, so they don't know if it can be fixed up and people move back in."

"The pawn shop and the cigar store, yeah. I know the place. I've bought cigarettes there, a small old fellow, hard of hearing, named Rocky. Do they know the cause of the fire yet, have you heard? I hope it's not arson."

"Actually," Sal said, "it might be. That's what's going around. But that's what's in people's heads these days after your place went up like Nagasaki. Everybody's jumping to conclusions."

"Then, why the pawn shop? And the cigar store? They don't sound like targets. It must have been somebody upstairs. Can you ask around as to who or what those upper-floor tenants were?"

"I'll try to find out. Maybe the firebug thought *you* had moved in upstairs, ha ha."

I tried to chuckle, but I wondered if, no joke, maybe somebody had.

I wasn't able to reach any other gay business owners, but I got lucky and caught Bobby Carletti at the end of a shift. He was about to head out from the precinct, and he said he was glad I had called.

"Clifford, as I live and breathe, can that really be you? The word around town is either you're holed up in New Hope with a chorus boy from the theater there, or somebody helped you take a flyer off the Camden bridge and we're all finally rid of you going around tossing stink bombs at judges and court clerks. I guess it must be the chorus boy, am I right? Is he really cute?"

I didn't know what it was about Bobby. He was actually kind of a jerk who could be endlessly annoying. Yet whenever he talked to me the way he did, my dick would get a little firm. I think it was because he was a real hunk and he loved sex, so I was willing to put up with a lot from him. Maybe someday I would become equally aroused by somebody sweet and decent like Amos Leary, the shoe-flogging chub at Wanamaker's who admired the German guy who argued that homosexuality was just another part of nature. At least it would be pretty to think I would.

I told Bobby I was working on something he didn't need to hear about, and because he would just get on my case, he really didn't. I said I was curious as to whether the police department was still being instructed by higher-ups to be making gay people's lives as miserable as possible.

"Yeah, that's the word," he said, his voice dropping confidentially. "Though the targeting is limited for some reason. Only parks and tearooms and what have you. Stem and Polly-Wolly's are shut down, and the word is we are *not* supposed to bother The Rooster or Nellie's Tavern. Of course, they're both owned by the Russo family, so what else is new?"

"I thought mob-owned bars were sometimes also hit, just for the sake of appearances. They get tipped off first. That's not true this time?"

"No, I've even whispered in the ears of a few acquaintances that if they want to go out and imbibe in public, they can do it at The Rooster or Nellie's and not to worry about getting arrested or even called mean names and shoved around. What's going on is kind of confusing, but that's all I can tell you."

"What about this fire last night on Cuthbert?" I asked. "It's not far from my building which burned down, and I hear that this one also looks like it was intentionally set."

"That's what the fire marshal says. But it's an odd situation. The upper floors of that building were empty. In June all the tenants had been given a month's notice to move out. A pawn shop and a cigar store were left, so what was going on there? I mean, go figure."

Nothing Bobby was telling me was clarifying anything. It was tempting to think of some reason to question him in person—and maybe go out and pick some corn and work up a fresh sweat for Bobby—but I had more pressing matters to settle.

I asked Bobby if he was heading home to take his boys to Little League practice, but he said no, he had done that the night before, and Wednesday was his bowling night. I knew what that meant. He'd leave his house with his bowling bag and team uniform but head straight into Center City and the rooming house on Spruce where he would meet a guy. Sometimes the guy was me. I said I hoped that he had a good time tonight and that he didn't drop his bowling ball on his dick. He said he never had yet.

CHAPTER 44

It was eight o'clock and the sun was down, and still no word from Lucas Quayle. This was bad. I listened to the radio news for any report of a husband and wife found dead in the river. WCAU was just, a GI held captive by the Russians in Korea was from Palmyra.

Why was Quayle not calling? He knew I was staying with Lathrop in Quakertown and that was how to reach me. I could think of no reason he was failing to phone except he was forcibly being prevented from doing so. I felt bad for his frightened wife, the thin blonde in her tennis whites and a fortifying beverage in her sun-tanned hand.

I enjoyed one of those helpful fluids myself while Lathrop fixed a late supper of grilled wienies, fresh corn, and juicy tomatoes, a Pennsylvania summer feast fit for the gods. I felt sad for Lathrop, too, when he told me that he was unsure if he would be able to stay on the farm. His corn and potato crops only paid the bills in summer. The rest of the year he had been a substitute teacher in the high school. But he had been dropped from that list when some parents had complained that their kids were being taught by a communist.

"A homo commie, or just a commie?" I asked.

"Just commie was enough."

"But you're not a real Red."

"It was an organization I was in in college. The FBI put it on a list, and somebody found out."

"What was the organization?"

"The Lewisburg branch of MFA—Medicine for All. We were trying to get the government to pay for everybody's doctor and hospital bills."

"That is kind of communistic. But firing you from your teaching job is ridiculous."

Lathrop gave me one of his looks meaning he was never sure how to answer my opinions and went back to getting supper on the table.

After we ate, I had a smoke, and then soon another one. I stared at the phone practically nonstop, but that didn't help.

To pass the time, Lathrop played some Pete Seeger records, songs about the Spanish Civil War. I didn't know about the battles the songs were referring to, but Lathrop did and he sat in a trance listening to these tunes. I wondered if Lathrop's radio could pick up the New Orleans jazz station, but it would have been impolite to suggest taking him away from these records that meant so much to him. I was all for Truman, but I didn't think there was a type of music connected with him. His daughter sang opera, but with Harry it was maybe "Happy Days Are Here Again." Pete Seeger probably thought a song like that was piffle.

At midnight, still no call. I had gone through more of the Jim Beam than I ought to have. I was running out, in fact, and wondered if there was a state store in Quakertown that I could make a run to in the morning. Lathrop said I'd have to go all the way to Doylestown, and I said, "Who the hell is running Bucks County, Carrie Nation?"

I was grateful that *they*, the sinister and deadly *they*, were not showing up at the farm that night, because I was in no condition. Lathrop had had a few himself. He drank some kind of mineral water bottled upstate that he laced with vodka, and the drink smelled like the inside of a limestone cave. My bourbon smelled warm and caressing and produced exactly that effect. It was the boyfriend I otherwise didn't seem to have at the moment.

At 1 a.m., the phone hadn't rung, and I told Lathrop I was going up to hit the hay. He had a spare room upstairs with a decent mattress and some cross-ventilation plus a fan.

Lathrop said he'd stay by the phone for a while, and his records would help keep him from dozing off. They would have had the opposite effect on me, but I didn't say so.

I was out cold within seconds, and didn't dream of suicides, or murders, or arsons, or "history," or *lists*, as best as I can recall. I was as good as brain dead.

Lucas Quayle did not call that night, or in the morning, either. But he was very much alive, it turned out, and the next day he contacted Lathrop and me in the most unexpected way of all.

CHAPTER 45

Breakfast was painful. My head felt as if fag-bashing goons from PPD had done a job on it. My mouth tasted like I'd spent an intimate night with Joe Stalin. Even my neck hurt; what did that mean?

Lathrop let me make the coffee Egyptian-style. He cut his with a lot of milk and sugar, but I took mine like a man. We each had toast but nothing else.

He had spent the night on a daybed near the phone downstairs. I asked him whether, if it had rung, would he have heard it, given his condition? He told me he thought so. He said he hadn't been as bad off as I had been, and that was not hard to believe.

We sat on the back porch and drank our coffee, and I smoked. By nine o'clock I had pretty much concluded that Lucas and Carolyn Quayle were dead. I imagined their daughters' grief. The two girls were away at tennis camp, and who would break the news? Who would look after them? What other family members were there to take them in?

Was I somehow responsible for what had happened to the Quayles? I was up to my receding hairline in this whole thing, and if I had done something differently—as I had not done in the case of Leslie Croyer—would the Quayles still be alive?

I managed to tell myself that that kind of thinking was hooey, or borderline hooey, and I almost started to believe that Lucas Quayle had chosen to involve himself in the Judge Stetson-extortion-wife-beating-gangster-list-"history" situation, and whatever the terrible consequence had been were entirely his own doing.

By midmorning I was ready to function again, but function how and why and to what end? I was feeling frantic but at the same time helpless, a turtle on its back, a beached whale, a trumpet player at Minton's with a busted lip. I had no idea where to turn next.

And then everything changed in an instant.

Lathrop and I heard Mrs. Hockenberry's car pull up out front with the mail. He went out to collect it and came back into the house exclaiming excitedly.

"It's a letter from Lucas Quayle! He's okay."

"No shit."

"This was mailed yesterday. He doesn't say where he's staying, just gives a number to call. But the postmark on the envelope is Lord's Valley."

"He's in heaven? Jesus, let me have a look."

"Not heaven. The Poconos. It's a small town not far from Milford. I know it."

I read the letter aloud:

Dear Bill and Clifford,

I hope this gets to you on Thursday. Normally the mail is overnight, the postmaster up here says, but with the U.S. Mail you never know.

Carolyn and I are near our daughters' tennis camp in Pike County. You might be familiar with this rural area, a bit west of Milford.

The both of you were probably concerned about Carolyn and me, and I am sorry I was not able to get in touch sooner. The thing is, I have reason to believe, Bill, that your phone has been tapped. I now know that Tom's was. As a precaution, you should be very careful who you talk to on your home phone and what you talk about.

I have an idea of how to get us all out of this horrendous situation we find ourselves in, and it is best if we meet face to face so you can hear my strategy. If you receive this letter on Thursday, please call me at noon at the number at the bottom of the page. It's a pay phone nearby, and before I take this letter to the post office I'll include the number.

I think you both understand the seriousness of what we are all coping with here.

As I know you have figured out by now, my family is at the center of this nightmarish situation involving a very great deal of money and a good number of people, some of them innocent, but quite a few of them totally corrupt and even violent.

If I don't hear from you today at noon, I'll assume the mail was delayed and I'll hope to receive your call tomorrow.

Good luck to you, and to all of us, and to all decent, law-abiding people in Southeastern Pennsylvania.

Lucas Quayle

Written in pencil at the bottom of the letter was a phone number in the town of Lords Valley.

"He sounds confident," Lathrop said. "As if he has a way to end the mayhem and danger. And restore the gay Philly status quo? Maybe even with Judge Stetson reined in? Though he doesn't say that."

"And he also doesn't mention who he thinks is tapping your phone. If it's true, I don't think that's The Hat or Ray Phipps. It sounds like the FBI."

"It could be that some fed thinks I'm a Russian agent, like the high school principal does. But I doubt if J. Edgar Hoover has me listed as a Soviet spy, so maybe not. I have Russian sympathies, but I'm not quite a traitor."

"Are you really sympathetic to the Russians? Wow, Bill."

"I was being sarcastic. Even Pete Seeger is over the Soviet Union."

"You left-wingers have such a dry sense of humor. Which actually I kind of like. Anyway, it's almost eleven. Where is there a phone we can use to call Quayle in an hour?"

"At the drugstore in Quakertown. There's an enclosed booth there."

As we drove towards Quakertown in Lathrop's old rattletrap Ford pickup, I kept trying to reconstruct in my mind who I had called on Lathrop's maybe wiretapped telephone and what we had talked about. And I wondered if my phone had been tapped, too, and if so, since when?

CHAPTER 46

We hadn't gone far when a black Dodge pulled out from some trees and began to follow us. Coincidence maybe, but it stayed about fifty feet behind. When the car didn't deviate at all, I made myself forget about the wiretap and kept an eye on this vehicle. Lathrop was driving the pickup truck, which made grinding noises when he shifted gears, not a good sign. I tried to make out who was driving the Dodge but could discern only two indistinct figures in the front seat.

In town, the Dodge parked not far behind us when we went into the drugstore. It was almost twelve, and several people were seated at the soda fountain counter ordering or having lunch. A tiny old lady with her hair in a bun was digging into a wet-walnut sundae. I picked up its maple syrup scent as we walked past the oldster on the way to the phone booth.

Lathrop had brought along a small collection he had of nickels, dimes and quarters, and he dropped some in the slot when the operator said Lords Valley for three minutes would be seventy-five cents.

When Lucas Quayle answered, Lathrop handed me the receiver as he eased out of the booth and I eased in.

"Where are you calling from?" Quayle asked.

"The Rexall drugstore in Quakertown."

"That should be safe enough. Do you have any indication that you are being watched or followed?"

"Yes, a black Dodge possibly."

"Can you lose it and drive up here?"

"Sure."

"Just make sure nobody is following you. These people are goons. They're mob people, and we have to keep them at bay until I can set my plan in motion."

"Mob people?"

"They tried to grab me in Elkins Park, and I had to use my mother-in-law's gun on them."

"The derringer she carried in her reticule."

"I don't think I hit any of them, but now I'm sure they are royally pissed off. I spoke with my business partner, Art Pudlow, and found out these thugs also apparently trashed our house in Doylestown. I think not long after I picked Carolyn up. I am so relieved she wasn't still there. All I need now is a little time, and maybe some help from you. I think if you can help protect me and Carolyn for another couple of days, we'll all be home free. I mean, relatively speaking free."

"Bill and I are curious as to what you have in mind."

The operator asked for another fifteen cents. I signaled to Lathrop and he handed it over, and I dropped the coins in the slot, *ka-ding ka-ding*.

"It's all quite major," Quayle said. "Historic even. That's why so many people are desperate to have it go their way."

"That's what your dad told me."

"My father is a troubled man. And morally weak, I'm sorry to say. He has some really awful ideas about a lot of important things. I'm more like my mom in my ways of thinking, though I'll never in a million years have what it takes to be the Quaker she was. I just hope all this can be dealt with—especially Uncle Harold—without Dad getting hurt too badly. Or ruined financially. In that regard, he's in rough shape as it is. Anyway,

I'll explain everything when I see you. Can you get up here later this afternoon?"

I said I could and I was very eager to hear both Quayle's explanations and about his, as he put it, "strategy" and "plan." He asked if we could meet at a tavern called Pete's Place just outside of Lords Valley on Route 739 at four o'clock. I said Lathrop and I would be there.

After I hung up, I repeated all this to Lathrop and asked him, "Does Quakertown have a taxi service?"

"Town Taxi, Ed Rathgeber."

"Is there a garage where you have your truck worked on?"

"Quakertown Esso."

Lathrop brought out another nickel and called Ed Rathgeber. We drove over to the Esso Station, where Lathrop consulted with the owner and then drove his truck into the vacant bay with us in it. The black Dodge was now parked across the road. We climbed out of the truck and walked out the back door of the Esso station. Ed Rathgeber was waiting there. We crouched down in the back seat of the taxi as Ed pulled out onto the highway and drove off. The black Dodge stayed put.

CHAPTER 47

The Plymouth was feeling the strain. When the taxi had dropped us off back at the farm, I didn't take time to check the radiator. We needed to hit the road north before the mob thugs, as Quayle had described them, figured out that we had given them the slip. We grabbed a few items—bread, peanut butter, cigarettes, the requisite beverages—and sped away, though with the Plymouth, "sped" is a term to be used loosely.

I filled the radiator—and the watering can in the back seat—at a service station in Leithsville, where we also picked up some cold pop. The sun was again beating down. I wondered if it would add even more blisters to the old tin can's hood and roof. The car had survived the incineration of my office building, but now it was as if I was expecting it to carry two people across the desert from Cairo to Khartoum, a task too cruel.

The hills were the worst, and as we got up into the Poconos there were a lot of them. Downhill wasn't bad, but uphill sometimes made the machine rhumba, even without the Ted Weems orchestra. The music on the radio didn't help—Mickey Mouse bands and Arthur Godfrey singing "The Too Fat Polka." The Plymouth didn't want to polka.

We stopped a couple of times to give the car a rest and to piss in the woods, but we still managed to cover the ninety-one miles in under three hours, arriving in Lords Valley at ten to four.

Pete's Place was easy to find, just outside of town on the main road west towards Blooming Grove. It was a low, dark wooden structure with a neon Iron City Beer sign in one small window and a Schlitz sign in the other. A couple of cars were parked out front, and I guessed that the shiny purple Oldsmobile that looked like a big eggplant with a grill was Lucas Quayle's.

He was seated alone in a shadowy corner booth. He had a half-full Coke bottle in front of him and the rest of the Coke in a glass with some ice cubes. The only other person in the bar was a middle-aged guy in a suit and tie on a stool in conversation with the barkeep. Quayle stood up to shake hands. He and Lathrop had not actually met before, their sole connection being Tom Heimer.

Lucas Quayle looked a little like his father, Parsons, chiseled and lanky, with a steady cornflower blue gaze, but younger and fitter. He was in pressed khakis and a dress shirt like his pop's, except not frayed at the edges. Also, Quayle was oddly odorless, and I realized here is a man who does not smoke. Did Quakers not use tobacco? I tried to imagine the William Penn statue on top of City Hall puffing on a pipe but couldn't.

As soon as I tagged Quayle as a nonsmoker, my mouth started watering. "Mind if I smoke?"

"Not at all."

Lathrop and I both lit up.

"I guess we're lucky to be all in one place," I said. "Even lucky to be alive."

"I don't think they were ever going to kill me," Quayle said. "On account of my father's involvement. Everybody is ticked off at Dad because he gave me a copy of the list of investors, but they also know he's kind of a wild card in all this because he knows about Harold Stetson's terrible behavior toward Aunt Mae. I think I was supposed to be beaten up and frightened

193

away from interfering with what they're doing. But they've got these mob guys from the Russos that they have let loose, so who knows? Obviously they killed Tom, and I have to face the fact that I am partially responsible for that."

He took a deep breath and swigged from his Coke. I had three dozen questions, but I waited for him to go on.

Looking at me, Quayle said, "I actually don't understand why you are still among the living, Clifford. Other than myself, they have been merciless with anybody who got in their way. After I told Tom about Uncle Harold and about the list and he began to interfere, they threw him in the river. Then they somehow found out that you were also prepared to muck things up for them. I'm guessing your phone was tapped along with Tom's and Bill's. But they didn't kill you, and I have no idea why. All I can say is, somebody somewhere must be looking out for you."

"I can't imagine who," I said. "Of course, they did burn down my office. And they've been following me around whenever possible and giving me a major case of the heebie-jeebies."

"What was happening was, both of you guys were being seriously and dramatically warned off, and I have to say I'm grateful to you for not heeding those warnings."

"So," I said. "Lucas. Cough it up. Spill the beans. Tell all. *What in the bloody hell is going on here?*"

The bartender and his customer glanced our way.

Quayle smiled weakly. "You haven't figured it out? I'm surprised. Given the location of your office."

"Former office would be the more accurate way of putting it."

"Exactly. What's behind your burned-down office on Cuthbert Street, Clifford? What's in back of the buildings with those gay bars, Stem t' Stern and Polly-Wolly's?"

"Physically behind them? An alley. And then the railroad."

"And where is the railroad? It's up on the Filbert Street

viaduct, more commonly referred to as the Chinese Wall. That wall is coming down. Broad Street Station is coming down. The Pennsylvania Railroad is in the direst of dire financial straits, and it is finally going to consolidate its operations at Thirtieth Street Station and at Suburban Station. A brand spanking new Philadelphia Center City is soon to be born. And with it, a chance for certain people in the know to make a whole, whole, *whole* lot of money."

We stared at him. Lathrop said, "The demolition of the Chinese Wall has been in the works for twenty years, but it's still there. I have to say, I have my doubts about it going anywhere soon."

"I can see why," Quayle said. "Everybody has hated that hideous wall almost from the day it was put up. It was going to be demolished, but first the Depression happened, and then the war. Now the coast is clear and the railroad is ready to deal. With the wall gone, downtown will be completely rebuilt. Imagine what that means. A grand boulevard! Office towers! Apartments! Restaurants! New pocket parks! A few people got tipped off that the wall was coming down and rounded up some friends to invest in the redevelopment. But first, naturally, it would help if real estate prices in the wall area tanked and the investors could buy up, on the cheap, the old buildings that will be torn down to make way for the new ones. So we've had arsons, and we've had nasty campaigns to shut down the gay businesses. Just a bit of softening up to pave the way for buyers prior to the announcement of the birth of a new Philadelphia for the ultramodern, postwar twentieth century. The investors aren't merely going to make a killing; they're going to make history. And believe me, there is no stopping them. They *will* do it."

Uncle Grant's voice spoke to me inside my head: *You can't stop progress.*

It was Lathrop who now said aloud the obvious. "And Judge Stetson is one of the investors?"

"One of seventeen."

I said, "They can name the new highway Hat Boulevard."

"There is no putting a halt to this thing," Quayle went on. "It's too big, too necessary. Everybody who counts agrees. The Republican city machine. The Democrat reformers who want to take over city government. Even the FBI helped out, probably at the behest of Uncle Harold. They were tapping Tom's phone anyway, on account of his teachers union activities, and Tom believed that's how they found out he was going to try to expose Uncle Harold as both a wife beater and a participant in a violent campaign to roll up Center City real estate on the cheap. Tom saw that he could take down not only a sadist and an extortionist but also a man who was part of a murderous conspiracy. That made him too dangerous to remain among the living."

My head was swimming. I said, "So you told Tom about The Hat being a wife beater and also about his involvement in the redevelopment scheme with its gay club attacks and beatings and arsons?"

Quayle grew even more solemn. "I did. I supposed Tom would go to the newspapers or . . . I don't know what. I knew he was the type of left-winger who would—would find a way. I knew he couldn't stop the redevelopment project, and I didn't really want him to, but I hoped he'd at least be able to expose the illegality."

"How did you know about the campaign of violence?" I asked. "Your dad told you about the investors. Did he also admit to all the rough stuff?"

Quayle shook his head sorrowfully. "I suspected what was going on, and when I asked him, he said, oh sure, why the hell not? Then when I acted shocked, which God knows I was, Dad said, 'Why do you care? It's mostly a bunch of damned fairies who are affected! And you're not one of those—at least so far as I know, you're not.'" Quayle blinked once but did not elucidate further on that point.

Lathrop and I sat there trying to digest this wild tale. Wild, but with us knowing Philly's post-Benjamin Franklin checkered financial and social and political history, not at all far-fetched. Still, one thing I didn't get.

"So if all this tearing down and building up and making money hand over fist is set in concrete, what do you have in mind to change? I mean, what exactly are the three of us doing here?"

So then he laid it out.

CHAPTER 48

First, Quayle explained to us why he had gotten involved at all. When, after a few cocktails, his father had admitted to Lucas how Harold Stetson regularly beat Parsons's sister Mae black and blue, the peaceable and decent-natured Lucas, who had a streak of his Quaker pacifist mother in him, wanted to confront the judge and tell him if he didn't stop doing this, Lucas would report him to the Montgomery County sheriff or, if that got no result, the state Judicial Conduct Board. Parsons pleaded with his son to stay out of it. He said if Harold was mad at Parsons he would keep him from being one of the investors in the Center City project, and having lost most of the family money in the crash in 1929, Parsons needed money to live comfortably (his Cricket Club membership was mentioned) and to leave something behind for his granddaughters. This was also the occasion when Lucas's father confessed about, almost bragged about, the mob-managed wave of violence the investors had set in motion.

It was then that Lucas came up with a different approach to at least fix The Hat's wagon. "I was determined to do something to get that guy," he told Lathrop and me. "The other reason I really wanted to get Uncle Harold out of the courtroom was the way he treated homosexuals. I am not prejudiced, and I knew that Tom became homosexual after college, and I would never hold that against him. He had told me about how gay people were blackmailed and extorted by Uncle Harold and his court clerk, Ray Phipps. If I could help put a stop to that despicable practice, I wanted very much to do so. And I knew Tom was the way to make it happen."

If Lucas had been drinking something stronger than Coke, would he have told this story differently? Mention that he'd had sex with Tom in college? Anyway, I gave the guy credit. I knew a lot of men who were sometimes "that way" under certain circumstances, but otherwise were mean and stupid in the way they went around talking about homosexuals. Quayle was the opposite, even if he bent his personal facts a wee bit while discussing this topic.

"Good for you, Lucas," I said, and Lathrop nodded. Lathrop and I did not look at each other.

"Here's my idea," Quayle said. "I don't know if there's a way to keep Uncle Harold from becoming even richer than he is from the new development project. Milk and Honey is what the investors are calling it. But at the very least I think I can keep him from hurting Aunt Mae any more. This is the place where you come in, Clifford. Dad told me there's a nurse at Norristown Hospital who treated Aunt Mae after her husband broke her nose a couple of years ago. This nurse didn't believe Mae's story about falling in the bathroom. She was also bruised all over, and the nurse urged Mae to contact the police.

"Aunt Mae is so totally under the control of Uncle Harold, though—scared and intimidated and dependent—that she won't do anything about him. She's also religious and told Dad the Bible says wives are supposed to submit to their husbands, no matter what. It is all so tragic and, to me, infuriating."

"I've seen other cases like that," I said.

He nodded. "So you know how it is. I'm going to hire you to meet with this nurse—I've already spoken with her briefly—and

199

locate any medical records detailing this incident and any other records that might prove there were other incidents."

I listened to this with a sinking feeling. Quayle was so sincere, and so terribly naïve.

"Then," he said, "we go to the Montgomery County district attorney with the evidence. And the esteemed Judge Harold Stetson of Philadelphia Superior Court is charged with assault and battery. The Judicial Conduct Board will force him off the bench pending a full investigation. The old reprobate will never recover his reputation. And just possibly he'll be convicted of a felony. Don't you think approaching it like that makes sense? That it has a better than even chance of working?"

I lit another Lucky.

"Who," I asked, "is actually filing a charge against Judge Stetson? The nurse can't do it. Only your aunt can."

"I hope," he said, "that once the police interview Aunt Mae she'll see that she is not alone in her pain and humiliation, and she'll be persuaded to break free of Uncle Harold's evil control. I know doing it this way is not a sure thing, but I can't think of any other way. Can you?"

"Not offhand."

Lathrop asked, "Do you have cousins? Do Harold and Mae have their own children?"

"They had a little boy, Kendrick, who died in the 1918 flu epidemic. Their daughter, Sarah, committed suicide in 1932. She had had mental problems from when she was a child. So there hasn't really been anybody close enough to Aunt Mae to help her break free from her sadistic husband. I think she might have a few friends who suspect what has been going on, but they don't seem able to influence her either, if they have even tried. People of our background don't tend to talk openly about things like this."

We sat for a minute or so not speaking. Now I could just barely make out over behind the bar a radio broadcasting in low volume not a Phils game but, of all things, a Yankees game. This was Pennsylvania, and what kind of bullshit was this? I might as well have been back in Egypt.

I said to Quayle, "We can try it. But to be honest, I don't think it's likely to work."

His nice face drooped. "Why? Because you think Aunt Mae is too far gone? Too old to change? To break free?"

"In my experience, battered wives are so beaten down physically and mentally they rarely find the strength to leave their husbands. They live with it, like your aunt."

Uncle Grant's voice: *The old gal is set in her ways.*

"We have to try," Quayle said. "I have the name of the nurse, and I know she's still at Norristown Hospital. And there's somebody I went to school with in the Montgomery County DA's office. So we could actually know in a couple of days if this is going to work. Just letting Uncle Harold know what we're up to might get him to call off these gangsters who are scaring the daylights out of us and who knows how many other people that The Hat and his cohorts feel threatened by."

I thought, well, maybe while I dug into this nurse thing, I'd think up some better way of dealing with—"history" is what we were now calling it.

"My fee," I said, "is forty-five dollars a day, plus expenses. Can you handle that?"

"Of course. I am far from wealthy, but my brokerage provides an adequate livelihood, and my wife has assets. It's her grandmother's house we're living in in Doylestown."

Except for my now being in a position to pay my next phone bill, this whole thing looked borderline hopeless, or did until the words Quayle spoke next.

"One thing that might help is the list of seventeen investors in the development project. It's possible one or more of these men has enough of a social conscience to object to Uncle Harold's tactics. Tom was planning to use the list to try to leverage anti-

Hat activity. That's why he became such a grave danger to the top investors, and they had to stop him any way they could. They knew from the wiretaps how determined Tom could be."

Quayle retrieved from his pants pocket a single folded piece of paper and handed it to me.

He said, "Perhaps there's even someone among the seventeen you have access to or even know."

I thought, *fat chance.* Then I looked at the name at the top of the investors' list. If I hadn't had a Lucky Strike between my lips, my jaw would have dropped. Suddenly a lot of what had happened over the past eleven days became glaringly, even frighteningly, clear.

CHAPTER 49

Mike Stover.

He was the top investor at a cool ten mil, and the so-called "chairman" of the Milk and Honey group. Which meant any rough stuff had to have been okayed by him at least in a general sense. *Do what needs to be done, and don't tell me about it.*

Seeing his name at the top of the list, I felt physically sick to my stomach with disgust. I had known the guy was a hard-ass—but *this?*

At the same time, seeing his name, I thought I might yet make all this work out well enough, at least for my fellow queer-as-a-two-dollar-bill Philadelphians.

I scanned the rest of the list. Some of the other names were familiar to me from reading the paper, but I had no connection with any of them. There was a cardboard box tycoon, a shipping magnate, a construction company owner, two heads of banks, two real estate moguls, a couple of other big-money guys, and of course Judge Harold Stetson. In for smaller amounts were court clerk Ray Phipps, two congressmen—one Republican, one Democrat—and at the bottom of the list, Parsons Quayle, let in, according to his son, to keep him from ratting out his wife-beater brother-in-law. The Russo family was not mentioned, and I wondered who on the list was fronting for the mob. The shipper? The box manufacturer? One of the congressmen?

As Lathrop and I headed back south, it was no longer so ferociously hot. We still had all the windows rolled down on the Plymouth, which was complaining less often than it had earlier in the day. But at a quarter to six the heat was only just tiresome instead of all but intolerable.

We had to yell over the racket of the wind rushing through the car, and I kept asking Lathrop to repeat things. Was my hearing going? Grandma Waterman had lost hers, but she was in her seventies. I was only forty-three and quite a fine specimen except for some sprouting love handles. When I mentioned these to Bobby Carletti, he said, yeah, Cliff, you have four love handles, the ones at your waist plus your two ears—North Philly homo wit.

I told Lathrop about my two encounters with Mike Stover— the earlier one with his kid and the Pekingese and the one with the crustless sandwiches out in Broomal—and how I now believed that it must have been Stover who told the investment powers-that-be that I was a threat, Stover having learned from the FBI wiretaps on Tom and then on Bill Lathrop—and on me?—of my involvement and determination. Trevor Dunlap had no doubt been the conduit for what had been gleaned from the taps. It was why people like Nelson Miller, Polly-Wolly's owner, and Bobby Carletti had warned me that there were cops out to hurt me, and why my office burned down.

"A two-faced, double-dealing big-businessman," Lathrop said. "Why am I not surprised?"

And why was I not surprised Lathrop put it that way? And why was I not surprised when I thought, yeah, well, maybe capitalists are as untrustworthy as Reds? Which left us all with . . . what?

Quayle and his wife were going to stay at an inn near Lords Valley until I could report back because they felt sure they would be safe there. Quayle said he still had his mother-in-law's derringer with him, and he thought it still had a few shots left in it. I was impressed by his quickly acquired firearm skills, such as they were. He was all of a sudden Doylestown's Quaker gunslinger and the fastest draw in Elkins Park.

Lathrop, we decided, would be wise to also hide out for a few days. He phoned a friend in Bethlehem he could stay with, and I dropped him off there. He said his corn buyers would be annoyed, but it was best to avoid the black Dodge people until I could have a word or three with Mike Stover.

I didn't need to avoid Philly, on account of I apparently had a protector and I knew who he was. So I managed to get the fuming and wheezing Plymouth back into the city just after ten and stash it behind Sal's.

Sal's was empty except for a couple of guys I didn't know. Sal wasn't there either, only his sidekick Mario who told me things were so quiet he might shut down early and go home.

Home sounded like just the ticket, and I dragged my sorry butt over to Locust. My building was still standing. I opened the windows, got the fans churning, and took a cold shower. I walked around in the altogether, admiring myself when I passed a mirror, mentally skipping over two items. There wasn't much to eat in the fridge, but I'd had a quick ham sandwich in Bethlehem when I dropped off Lathrop, so I made do with a serving of Jim Beam, a cigarette, and the stack of Coleman Hawkins records. "Body and Soul" was first and last, and while I listened, I found myself becoming teary-eyed with deep contentment and, whenever I let myself contemplate what I had to do over the next few days, a certain level of fear.

CHAPTER 50

How had I let this happen? The Clifford Waterman I thought I knew was not the Clifford Waterman who was up to his neck in this—Jewish people had a word for it, *mishigas*. For a long time, I had pretty much plainly understood what I was able to do and what I was not able to do. A healthy respect for your own limitations is the byword of a person who plans to live to a ripe old age and sit on his porch swing and enjoy a glass and a smoke. I had survived both the army and the police, and those should have provided lessons enough for any intelligent grown-up, which statistically I was.

Driving over to Norristown in the morning traffic, I daydreamed about chucking the whole business and then hoped my car lasted long enough for me to drive it down The Hat Boulevard. The hell with it all. Not my problems. But obviously that would mean leaving a number of excellent human beings in the lurch, and anyway Philly gay guys' problems *were* my problems, me being one of the town's most notorious cocksuckers.

I could hear Uncle Grant: *Lie down with dogs, get up with fleas*. But no, this time that didn't sound right. I needed to have a talk with Amos Leary again. He had a mixed-up outlook that was half crazy and half sane that I liked. Also, I had in mind a way Amos could be of practical assistance in my current endeavors, if he was willing.

I had reached Mike Stover's tire company office by phone at nine, and fifteen minutes later his secretary called me back and said Mike would like me to drive out to his house in Broomal at four that afternoon if it would be convenient. I said it would.

I had also called the Norristown Hospital nurse, Millie Styles, the potential witness who had wanted to report Harold Stetson for wife-battery. It took a while to get her on the phone. I had to say it was a family emergency, and she was plenty miffed at first. But when I hastily explained why I wished to speak with her, she cooled down and said sure, she had an early lunch break at eleven and I should meet her at the hospital's main entrance.

There was a drugstore across the street from the hospital that had a vacant booth at this early hour for lunch, and we grabbed it and ordered tomato soup for Millie and a ham salad on whole wheat for me.

She was sixty or so, squat and busty with attentive dark eyes, and her uniform was Rinso white. Her cap was so starched it looked as if it would have survived being rammed by the Titanic.

"I've sometimes wondered," she said, "whether anybody would ever take notice of what Mrs. Stetson was obviously suffering through and do anything about it. So it's her nephew Lucas who sent you to see me? I spoke with him on the phone earlier in the week. He told me how outraged he was when he learned from his father of this pattern of abuse that's apparently been going on for a very long time."

I said yes, it was Lucas I was working for. "He says he knows someone in the Montgomery County DA's office who might be willing to investigate and, Lucas hopes, persuade Mrs. Stetson to file charges. Lucas is hoping you would be willing to testify about the injuries you saw in the ER a couple of years ago and your professional opinion about how those injuries occurred."

She had ordered a cherry Coke and she stirred it with her

straw. "Did Mr. Quayle give you the name of whoever it is in the DA's office?"

"No, not yet. That was going to be my next step."

There was no need to tell Styles that I doubted this whole approach was going to lead anywhere at all, and anyway I had what I now believed to be a sounder plan.

"Well," she said, "I can't imagine which attorney or other worker in that office is supposedly this helpful and understanding person."

"I'm sorry to hear that."

"I've been an ER nurse for twenty-three years, and I know the signs by now. They are not subtle. Severe bruising, broken bones, facial trauma. The types of wounds and injuries that can't really have happened any other way except by being hit or kicked. In Mrs. Stetson's case, it was a broken nose, among numerous other bruises and abrasions." She stirred her Coke like it was an enemy. "Once in a great while a wife or girlfriend confesses to me or to the doctor what actually happened. But even then, the patient hardly ever wants to get the law involved. They're too emotionally dependent on the batterer, or too financially dependent. Or, in a lot of cases, they think that they had it coming, that they are the ones who are to blame."

"It's a wrong way of thinking," I said, "but I'm not surprised that it happens that way."

"Once or twice, we've had a patient who says 'call the police' and who means it. But I have to tell you, Mr. Waterman. I've never really seen a situation go anywhere from that point. The cops write it up as a domestic dispute. It's private, a family matter. And when it gets as far as the DA, it's the same. 'Are you sure you want to air your family's dirty linen in public? Are you sure you want your boyfriend to have a criminal record? You know he says he loves you.' I have never seen one of these cases go forward legally, not once. I told Mr. Quayle all this, but he didn't seem to want to hear it. I did say that if Mrs. Stetson pressed charges against the judge, I would testify as to what I witnessed in July of 1945."

Her soup and my sandwich arrived.

We chatted some more while we ate. She said all the cases of wife-battering are horrible to see, but it was especially galling that an actual judge would be one of the perpetrators getting away with this depraved crime.

I had had in mind a particular fate for Judge Stetson if I could possibly arrange it that afternoon, and now I added a second type of justice that I believed he deserved.

CHAPTER 51

After the Norristown lunch, I drove into Center City and went into a stationery store. I purchased a pack of business-size envelopes, some typing paper, and nine first-class, three-cent stamps. Lucas Quayle had forked over a retainer, so I was, as the song goes, rich as Rockefeller, at least for current practical purposes. Back in my apartment, I wrote out nine letters all saying the same thing, checked the phone book for addresses, addressed the envelopes, placed the letters inside, then sealed and stamped the envelopes.

Carrying the letters in a paper bag, I took a cab over to Wanamaker's—I had to be in Broomal at four and time was running out—and found Amos Leary in the shoe department. He greeted me cheerfully, and when he finished up with a customer he came over to where I had seated myself.

"I need to talk to you," I said.

"Then we have to make it look like I'm selling you shoes."

"Do you sell clodhoppers?"

Amos disappeared for a minute and then returned with a number of boxes. He proceeded to stuff my feet into a variety of heavy workman's shoes. I was grateful I was not a steamfitter who had to wear these encumbrances.

"Here's what's going on," I said. "I'm doing a civic good

deed, and I need a little help."

"What kind of good deed?" he asked warily.

"It has to do with The Hat, but other than that I can't really say more."

The eyebrows went up on Amos's big, round face. "Too bad you can't say. On that subject, I'd be all ears."

I noted that he had nicely shaped ears. "The chore I am asking you to perform is conditional."

"Oh? And what might those conditions be?"

"I am going to give you this bag I have here. I want you to keep it in a safe place."

"Sounds easy enough."

"The bag contains nine envelopes that are stamped and addressed. The envelopes contain letters to various people. I want you to mail those letters, but only if one of two things happens."

He laughed. "The mystery deepens."

"First, I call you or write you and say to you, mail the letters."

"I'm making a mental note."

"The other circumstance is, something bad happens to me and you hear about it, such as, for example, I am suddenly known to be deceased."

He gave me a look. "*For example?* What's that supposed to mean?"

"I'm doing something some bad people are very pissed off about. I think I can keep them from killing me, but they've already killed someone else who challenged them, so I want to be able to tell a man I am going to do some negotiating with that my death or even grievous bodily harm will trigger certain events. The main event would be, you mail these letters."

He looked startled. "My Lord!"

"Don't worry. The man I am going to negotiate with won't know it's you who will mail the letters. He'll have no idea who it is. Otherwise, what would be the point?"

Amos proceeded to lace up the gigantic shoe he had placed

on my left foot.

"This is an anti-Hat activity you are involved in?"

"It is. My hope is that soon you will read about the outcome in the paper. And, Amos, you will dance a jig—you and many hundreds of others—up and down Market Street."

He looked at me carefully. "It sounds like either that, or 'Body of Faggot Philadelphia Private Investigator Washes Up Near Marcus Hook.'"

"This is possible. Will you help me?"

After a moment, he shrugged. "Well, of course I'll do it. God, Clifford, you make it sound like you are up to your tits in some kind of historic event."

I said, "You have no idea."

CHAPTER 52

Stover seemed no more and no less glad to see me on this occasion than he had on any earlier ones. Still Steady-As-She-Goes Mike. Mister Unperturbed. Mister I Take Life's Vicissitudes As They Come. And he had to suspect I was about to become quite the life's vicissitude.

As he had eight days earlier, he greeted me at the big front door of his schist castle and led me through the dim house and out to the rear terrace. As previously, nobody else seemed to be home. No staff or servants, no wife. Perhaps the missus was in town doing four o'clock tea with the Crown Princess of Upper Furbludgistan.

There were no small sandwiches shorn of their crusts this time, but Stover did think to have in place glasses on a silver tray, a pint of Jim Beam, and for himself a chilled bottle of his favorite Argentinian beer.

He was in his golfing outfit again, and I supposed that since he had said he also had just arrived from the city, he was planning to play a round after our chat.

Seated and with glass in hand and cigarette lit, I said, "I know everything."

He raised his beer glass. "I doubt that."

"You're not as ruthless and cunning as the ex-Nazi

manufacturer of the beer you're drinking. But, boy, do you come close."

His expression didn't change, but something in his eyes showed that this registered. "That's quite harsh."

"When I came out here last week and asked for your help with Leslie Croyer being extorted by Judge Stetson, you realized how serious I was about getting into it with The Hat. You were afraid my mucking about in the Stetson swamp would turn up additional ugliness, such as that Stetson beats his wife, and this would come out and sully everybody else involved in the Milk and Honey project. So you made sure I was soon going to be warned off by the cops and by a gay bar owner. You knew I was a hardheaded realist with some hard knocks behind me who could be reminded to stay in his place and I would pretty much do as I was told."

"You're not only an investigator," Stover said mildly, "you also read minds. You should go on television."

"You were also afraid that I would uncover the way your investment group is using mob goons and arsonists and gay-bashing cops to drive down real estate prices west of Center City so you all can buy up property and make a killing when the big announcement is made about the wall coming down and a gleaming new Philly going up in its place."

He wasn't even blinking, and I briefly wondered if Stover had had a fatal stroke and I was wasting my breath. That would have been unfortunate. I was going to need Stover to achieve a number of results.

"The worst thing you did, Mike, was when you found out through Trevor Dunlap's spying on Tom Heimer and through the FBI wiretaps—on Heimer and Bill Lathrop and, I'm guessing, on me, too—that Heimer had the wife-beating goods on Judge Stetson which he found out from his old friend Lucas Quayle. You also knew from the taps that Heimer wasn't just going to nail the judge but that he was going to expose all kinds of criminal goings-on, like the arsons and organized fag-bashing and all the real estate price manipulation. So, feeling seriously threatened, you told, or you told someone else to tell, the Russo family thugs to go after Heimer and stop the guy in his tracks. That's when he ended up dead in the river. Gee, Mike. How does it feel? I guess as a businessman, you probably have been proud of being a kind of wheeler-dealer, killer-diller. But an actual murderer? I am guessing that that's a new one for you. What's it feel like?"

He had barely moved, but now he did start blinking from time to time. The human eye needs moisture, and Stover, whatever else he wasn't, was human.

He said, "They were meant to scare the shit out of—what was his name? Heimer? Certainly not kill him. I mean, Jesus!"

"Scare him by throwing him off the Delaware bridge? Yeah, well, no, I don't think so."

He wasn't drinking his beer now, merely twisting the glass this way and that way. He look at me gravely and said, "You know, I protected you."

"I figured that out. My mother will send you a card."

"What's-his-name also. Lathrop?"

"Tom's old friend."

"Also, Lucas Quayle. After Heimer died, I made it plain to Ray Phipps, our security chief for the project, that you all should be warned away but that there should be no more fatalities. And, thank God, there haven't been."

"There was at least one suicide. But that was The Hat's doing. You're a little bit off the hook on that one, Mike. Except, of course, the young man who killed himself by jumping off the bridge instead of being pushed off was Leslie Croyer. He was the fellow who couldn't afford to pay to have his disorderly-conduct-in-a-homo-bar charge expunged, and you refused to use your in with The Hat to help the kid out. I attended his funeral up in Lock Haven. It was heartbreaking."

"I can't dispute that that's a terrible shame. I am geuinely sorry I was unable to help."

I looked him hard in the eye. "Unable or unwilling? I mean, for chrissakes, Mike, you're the top banana in the whole Milk and Honey scheme. You're in it for ten million dollars. Are you sitting here telling me that that doesn't buy the freedom of one pathetic queer in Harold Stetson's courtroom? Please don't bullshit me. I've been in the army and I've been in the cops, and I really cannot take a single iota more of bullshit. Admit to me that you are a moral leper, and state that you are sorry."

He continued to stare.

When Stover didn't speak, I added, "More than an apology, I want a number of other things from you."

I wondered if he knew what I was going to say. Again, he gave no sign.

"First, I want the hoodlums and the cops called off around Philly. No more arsons, and I want the hounding of homosexuals dialed back to a normal amount. In fact, let's do away with that type of behavior entirely for a while. The cops won't be able to contain themselves indefinitely. I understand that, but please see what you can do. I'll start checking first thing tomorrow."

Stover almost smiled. He must have thought that maybe this was going to be easy.

"Second, of course, call off the mob goons entirely. All the Quayles should be left alone, and Bill Lathrop, and naturally I include myself in that set of instructions. Tell the Russos to go back to loan-sharking, truck hijacking, narcotics, and gambling. Okay? Done deal?"

His face was as expressionless as his several tons of Wissahickon schist.

"Also, you will see to it that all the wiretaps are disconnected. I take it that's Trevor Dunlap's department. He's being paid by Treasury but working for the investors, am I right?"

Stover sat frozen.

"And here comes the big one, Mike. Are you ready?"

I took a twitch in his right cheek as an affirmative answer.

"Judge Harold Stetson will leave the bench. He will retire, and so will his court clerk, Ray Phipps. I'm not saying they should get off the Milk and Honey investors list. That aspect of the situation is, what's the term? Outside my purview. But no more using the Philadelphia Superior Court as a criminal enterprise. You got me, Mike? As the Russos might say, *capiche?*"

He finally spoke. "That is totally . . . preposterous."

"No, it's just the way it is going to be. And anyway, I am not finished yet."

Suddenly he looked as if he was trying not to explode. I was glad he was not armed, or at least I assumed he wasn't.

"The other thing is, before the Russos depart the scene from Milk and Honey, I want them to snatch Judge Stetson and beat the shit out of him. Specifically, they will break his nose. And they will tell him that if he ever again lays a finger on his wife Mae, they will hear about it. And they will come back and toss him off the Delaware bridge. Did you get that straight, Mike? Did you hear what I said?"

Through gritted teeth, he said, "You don't know what you're doing. You simply have no idea what you are now in for."

"Yep, I do."

"No. Oh, no. This is so much bigger than you, Clifford. Frankly, I am stunned that a man who normally has his two feet planted solidly on the ground like you doesn't see that. You have always been so adaptable to the ways of the world. Now you are talking like a man who is totally detached from reality. What happened to you along the way? I am just . . . puzzled is too weak a word to describe it."

"So, Mike. Here's the situation. Everything I directed you to do must be done. And in a timely fashion, too. Say, a week from now for the judge to have stepped down and then soon after that land in the hospital following a fall at home?"

"Idiotic!"

"Idiotic, you say, but I say nuh uh. Here's what will happen if you do not follow my orders. And they *are* orders. Like I'm Sergeant Waterman and you are PFC Stover. If you refuse to do these things—or if anything bad happens to me in the meantime, or anything bad happens to me anytime between now and the year I start collecting Social Security—if anything at all goes wrong in my estimation, the following will take place."

His face was looking dangerously flushed under his golfer's tan while he sat there and took it.

I said, "My untimely demise or your failure to carry out my instructions will trigger nine letters being mailed. The letters are all identical. They describe everything you total assholes have been up to in your Milk and Honey project. I mean everything, including the arson, and the mob tactics, and Heimer's murder. The judge's wife-beating is described in the letters, as well as the name of a nurse who will testify against the judge if any prosecutor is willing to charge a jurist. I should say a *retired* jurist."

I could all but see the synapses snapping inside Stover's head, even through his narrowed eyes.

"The letters I have described will be sent, if need be, to the following recipients. 1. *The Philadelphia Inquirer.* 2. *The Philadelphia Evening Bulletin.* 3. *Time Magazine.* 4. *The New York Times.* 5. WCAU Radio and TV. 6. *The Daily Worker.* 7. Eugene Ormandy, conductor of the Philadelphia Orchestra. 8. *The Social Register.* 9. The King of Denmark, c/o His Palace, Copenhagen."

I watched his reaction and it was a beaut. "They—those people—those publications—they won't believe any of it. They—those people and those institutions know my reputation. And my wife's. They know this is all nothing but a big pile of—a total heap of horseshit!"

"Maybe some will be doubtful. Or their bosses will tell them to nix the story. But some will check it out, and there's a good chance the whole Milk and Honey scheme will unravel. Also, you might not know the story Congressman Lyndon Johnson down in Texas tells. An army buddy from Dallas told me about it. A Texas politician running for sheriff wants to spread the word that his opponent fucks pigs. His staff guy says, 'That's silly, that guy doesn't really fuck pigs.' The pol says, 'Yeah, that's true, but let's make him deny it.'"

Stover's mouth was hanging open a little, and a small dot of drool was about to dribble onto his chin.

I added, "The thing about you, Mike, is that you and your Milk and Honey cohorts really are a bunch of pig-fuckers. But now that is about to end."

CHAPTER 53

Monnie Hinkle was finally moving to France to be with his main honey, and also to play bebop all the time instead of just on Mondays.

So, one night in late September, we had a farewell supper of chicken and biscuits at Horn & Hardart's and then came over to my place for some fluids, smokes, and a smooch or twenty-five. It was still unseasonably warm and the windows were open. Down on Locust, a bunch of gay guys—I could hear them calling each other *girl* or *Mary*—were leaning against a car and hanging out, and every couple of minutes they'd crack up laughing.

Monnie and I got naked right away. It had been a while, and for an hour or so we enjoyed some slippery lovie-dovie, sometimes the beast with two backs, sometimes the beast with one back and one front. After everything else, it was a big relief to have a night of fun uninterrupted by suicides, murders, or buildings going up in smoke.

Afterward, we were able to pick up the New Orleans all-jazz station, and we lay there and listened to Lester Young and Johnny Hodges and the Duke. Monnie said Ellington got most of the credit, but a lot of his best stuff was arranged or even composed by Billy Strayhorn, who was gay as a paper hat. Like Monnie, Strayhorn also had an American Negro beau in Paris, a piano player who couldn't get enough work in New York.

We lay for a long time smoking and imbibing and chewing the rag, and Monnie told me how sorry he was that Tom Heimer had died. Tom had become something of an annoyance to Monnie, but he said they had had some nice times together, and he was shocked that someone that young would kill himself—if that was what happened. Monnie said he'd heard it might not have been suicide, and did I know anything about it? He knew I'd been trying to locate Heimer.

I wasn't sure how much to tell Monnie. Part of my deal with Mike Stover had been, he'd call off the mob and also the cops to whatever extent he could, he'd remove The Hat and Ray Phipps from public life, and I would keep my mouth shut so that the Milk and Honey project could move ahead. After all, wasn't it really time to get rid of that damned Chinese wall?

I told Monnie I'd heard the same thing about Heimer's death, that maybe it was murder.

"I wonder if we'll ever know," Monnie said. "Tom told me before he disappeared he was going to do something about Judge Stetson, and then all of a sudden he ends up a floater. That sounds like some kind of evil shit to me."

"It has to make you suspicious."

"The poor bastard didn't even live to see The Hat land on his ass in the bathtub and call it quits down at the court. It's kind of disgusting, though, that now there are people trying to get the courthouse named after Stetson."

"I'm going to suggest to somebody that that's a terrible idea," I said, and reached for a fresh Lucky.

"Who are you going to suggest it to?"

"I have somebody in mind."

"Who? Are you a friend of Governor Duff?"

"Yeah, the gov and I meet over at the homo rooming house on Spruce once a month."

Monnie laughed. He said he'd miss our times together, even

221

though his grandmother, he said, would be relieved, if she ever found out about us, that he was no longer lying down with a white devil. He invited me to take a boat over to Paris for a visit with him and his "sweet thing" of a boyfriend, Kenneth, but I said I doubted I could swing it in the foreseeable future.

I also spent a night a week or so later with Amos Leary. It was a little like being intimate with tapioca pudding, but I reminded myself that I *liked* tapioca pudding, and anyway I enjoyed listening to Amos talk.

Amos knew I had had something to do with The Hat's departure from the courthouse, and Ray Phipps's as well. I told him it was to his benefit that he didn't know more, and he went along with that. He could, of course, have steamed open one of the letters—the one addressed to *The Social Register* must have aroused his curiosity—and then he'd have known everything. But he didn't seem to have done this, Amos being a far more ethical person than I could call myself.

I didn't sleep with Byron Summerson. He was not at all appealing to me, and anyway I doubt he'd have been interested in a man in his forties showing signs of middle-age spread. I did meet him for lunch, though, one day in October at a place in Chestnut Hill where the waitresses were all over sixty-five and wore black and white maids' outfits.

"I see," he said, "that that horrid Judge Stetson has retired. That is such an excellent development for Philadelphia homosexuals. Naturally I am haunted by the idea that if he had chosen to leave the bench in early August instead of early September, Leslie Croyer would still be alive. Fate can be so cruel and so stupid. I know there is no point to my dwelling on this, but it is so terribly unfair, am I right?"

I agreed fate was unfair. I did regret not being able to tell Summerson that it was his hiring me to help Croyer escape the clutches of The Hat that set in motion the events that eventually led to Judge Stetson's so-called bathroom accident and his departing the bench.

"There is still a lot of deep sadness up in Lock Haven," Summerson said. "And the Croyers keep pestering Abigail to take the Flyer up for a visit."

My first thought was, *who is Abigail?* Then, *oh, right, Abigail Pabst, alias Beverly Andrews.* I said, "Maybe she should say she's decided to become a missionary. In Guatemala."

"The Croyers never said anything to Abigail about Leslie's name being in *The Inquirer* for getting arrested in a homosexual bar. Maybe they didn't see it, and I doubt anybody in Lock Haven would ever mention it to them."

"That was my impression of the place."

"And certainly Abigail would never say anything. She was very fond of Leslie and she really wants his parents to keep their love for their son in their hearts and not have it sullied."

What a crock. "Really, Byron? The Croyers's love for their son can only be maintained by perpetrating a gigantic fraud?"

He glared. "It's what Leslie wanted. Does that mean nothing to you?"

I thought of Amos's German lunatic who went around saying homosexuality was just another way of being human. I thought of making a few comments about that to Summerson. Maybe it would make some sense to him or maybe it wouldn't. But our poached eggs on toast arrived, and anyway, I was worn out. For the time being, I had had enough of all this, more than enough. I asked Summerson to tell me about his antique reticule business, and he was eager to fill me in.

I didn't see Summerson again after that, and I didn't see Bill Lathrop either, or any of the Quayles. I did read about Mike Stover in the papers, collecting a good citizenship award from the mayor. Several years after that, I saw a picture in the paper of his wife cutting the ribbon for the opening of the Michael and Gwendolyn Stover Performing Arts Center in one of the new office and apartment complexes that went up after the wall and

Broad Street Station had become ancient history.

It took a while, but I was able to get the army to replace my Certificate of Discharge Under Less Than Honorable Conditions. When I opened an office in one of the new buildings that went up on Cuthbert Street, I hung it on the wall.

ACKNOWLEDGMENTS

I first set foot in Philadelphia in the summer of 1947 at the age of eight. I rode the Flyer down from Lock Haven by myself and was met at Broad Street Station by my Uncle Dick, who worked for an insurance company, though I stayed with my Aunt Janie, a medical technician. The city was so thrilling to me that I talked about it for months, and my mother complained she got sick of hearing about it.

I figured out much later that Uncle Dick was gay. As far as I know, he never came out to anyone in the family except, apparently, my grandmother. She once blurted out a sentence that began, "After Dick and Frank broke up . . ." My sister Kathy remembers visiting Dick and Frank and their big black poodle at their house in suburban Haverford. I now own Dick's Mabel Mercer LPs, which I found in Kathy's basement after Dick died in 1993.

I wrote *Knock Off The Hat* partly out of curiosity about Uncle Dick's life. I would dedicate the novel to his memory, except he is not here to give his blessing to my mentioning his full name. He was a man of his time and he remains so.

This is a work of fiction and all the characters are made up. But I think I was able to accurately portray the time and place thanks to a number of books. The main one was *City of Sisterly and Brotherly Loves: Lesbian and Gay Philadelphia, 1945-1972,* by Marc Stein, University of Chicago Press, 2000; second edition Temple University Press, 2004. This is a remarkable compendium on all facets of GLBT life in 1940s Philly, including numerous interviews with men and women present at the time. I am grateful to Professor Stein for bringing it all to life for me.

Also of big help were these nonfiction books: *The Gay Metropolis: The Landmark History of Gay Life in America,* by Charles Kaiser, 1997; *Gay New York: Gender, Urban Culture, and the Making of the Gay Male World 1890-1940,* by George Chauncey, 1994; *Jeb and Dash: a Diary of Gay Life 1918-1945,* edited by Ina Russell, 1993; *Lush Life, a Biography of Billy Strayhorn,* by David Hadju, 1996; and *The History of the Pennsylvania Railroad,* by Timothy Jacobs, 1988.

Novels that evoked the era memorably for me were: *Dodging and Burning,* by John Copenhaver, 2018; *True Confessions,* by John Gregory Dunne, 1977; and *Living Upstairs,* by Joseph Hansen, 1993.

Thanks, too, to the estimable Michael Nava for his excellent editorial suggestions and support and, as always, to first reader, main squeeze, and—lucky for me—spouse-person Joe Wheaton.

I also wish to thank the city of Bangkok, Thailand, where most of this novel was written, for perfectly reproducing the climate of Philadelphia in August.

ABOUT THE AUTHOR

Richard Stevenson is the pseudonym of Richard Lipez, author of eighteen books, including the Donald Strachey Private Eye Series. A former editorial writer at *The Berkshire Eagle*, he currently reviews mysteries and thrillers for *The Washington Post*. His reporting, reviews, and fiction have appeared in *Newsday*, *Harper's Magazine*, *Redbook*, *The Boston Globe*, *The Atlantic*, and *The Progressive*, among others.

Between the years 2005 and 2008, Shavick Entertainment adapted four of the Donald Strachey novels into films for the LGBT television network Here! Additionally, four of Stevenson's Strachey mysteries were short-listed for the Lambda Literary Award for Gay Mystery, with *Red White Black and Blue* winning in 2011. Richard grew up and was educated in Pennsylvania, and taught in the Peace Corps in Ethiopia. He is married to sculptor and video artist Joe Wheaton and lives in Becket, Massachusetts.

AMBLE
PRESS

Amble Press, an imprint of Bywater Books, publishes fiction and narrative nonfiction by LGBTQ writers, with a primary, though not exclusive, focus on LGBTQ writers of color. For more information on our titles, authors, and mission, please visit our website.

www.amblepressbooks.com